Jon's hazel eyes were close to hers and she could feel warmth where he was touching her.

"I'm going to be right here, okay?" he said. "Your lifeline, like we talked about yesterday. Everybody needs one in this line of work."

Her lifeline. Yes, she needed someone to make sure she wasn't going under. Jon would do that.

As if he could read her mind he said, "I'll be right here. I won't let you go under."

Sherry took a breath and nodded. Okay, she could do this. At least she would try.

"I'm okay."

He kissed her on the forehead. "You're more than okay. You can do this."

"I hope so."

FULLY COMMITTED

JANIE CROUCH

To "my" Jon and Sherry: it has been such a joy for everyone
to watch the two of you fall in love. A beautiful romance
that books—mine or otherwise—would only hope to imitate.
May you forever live out Ed Sheeran's "Tenerife Sea."
I'll always think of you when I hear it.

ISBN-13: 978-0-373-74941-6

Recycling programs
for this product may
not exist in your area.

Fully Committed

Copyright © 2016 by Janie Crouch

All rights reserved. Except for use in any review, the reproduction or
utilization of this work in whole or in part in any form by any electronic,
mechanical or other means, now known or hereinafter invented, including
xerography, photocopying and recording, or in any information storage
or retrieval system, is forbidden without the written permission of the
publisher, Harlequin Enterprises Limited, 225 Duncan Mill Road,
Don Mills, Ontario M3B 3K9, Canada.

This is a work of fiction. Names, characters, places and incidents are
either the product of the author's imagination or are used fictitiously,
and any resemblance to actual persons, living or dead, business
establishments, events or locales is entirely coincidental.

This edition published by arrangement with Harlequin Books S.A.

For questions and comments about the quality of this book,
please contact us at CustomerService@Harlequin.com.

® and TM are trademarks of Harlequin Enterprises Limited or its
corporate affiliates. Trademarks indicated with ® are registered in the
United States Patent and Trademark Office, the Canadian Intellectual
Property Office and in other countries.

Printed in U.S.A.

Janie Crouch has loved to read romance her whole life. She cut her teeth on Harlequin Romance novels as a preteen, then moved on to a passion for romantic suspense as an adult. Janie lives with her husband and four children overseas. Janie enjoys traveling, long-distance running, movie watching, knitting and adventure/obstacle racing. You can find out more about her at janiecrouch.com.

Books by Janie Crouch

Omega Sector: Critical Response

Special Forces Savior
Fully Committed

Omega Sector

Infiltration
Countermeasures
Untraceable
Leverage

Harlequin Intrigue

Primal Instinct

CAST OF CHARACTERS

Jon Hatton—Behavior analyst and crisis management special agent for Omega Sector: Critical Response. He's been sent to Corpus Christi, Texas, to assist with a serial rapist case.

Sherry Mitchell—Forensic artist for the FBI. Currently on vacation in Corpus Christi as she works through the trauma of past cases.

Zane Wales—Corpus Christi detective. Assigned to work the case with Jon.

Captain Harris—Corpus Christi police captain. He's not thrilled to have a member of federal law enforcement here to oversee his case or his people.

Jasmine Houze—Most recent victim of the Corpus Christi serial rapist.

Frank Spangler—Corpus Christi detective and forensic artist for the county. Only months away from retiring and not interested in anyone telling him how to run an investigation.

Caroline Gill—Corpus Christi paramedic and Sherry's friend from college.

Sara Beth Carreker—Head nurse at the Corpus Christi Memorial Hospital.

Dr. Anna Rosemont—Head trauma physician at Corpus Christi Memorial Hospital.

Dr. Paul Trumpold—Doctor at Corpus Christi Memorial Hospital.

Steve Drackett—Director of Omega Sector: Critical Response.

Brandon Han—Brilliant Omega Sector: Critical Response profiler. Sent to help Jon with the case.

Liam Goetz—Part of the Hostage Rescue Unit of Omega Sector. Friends with Jon and Brandon.

Chapter One

Sherry Mitchell was pretty sure she was the only tourist on the beaches of Corpus Christi, Texas, wearing a long-sleeved shirt and jeans to try to help her relax. Especially since the late-afternoon heat was expected to spike toward one hundred degrees on this June day.

Granted, she was under a large, colorful beach umbrella that threw enough shade to protect her from a great deal of the sun's rays and the heat. She was from Houston—a Texas girl born and bred—so was perhaps a little more adjusted to the heat than some of the tourists used to more temperate climates. But she'd still received a couple of odd glances.

She had her bathing suit—a red bikini she'd bought last week especially for this vacation—on under her clothes. Somehow she hadn't been able to force herself to wear just the tiny scraps of cloth just yet.

Not that they were *that* tiny. The suit itself was

pretty modest compared to some seen around here on any given day. Not to mention, it was quite attractive on her.

The problem wasn't anything to do with a bathing suit or modesty or appearances at all. The problem was the iciness that seemed to have permeated Sherry's very core recently.

She felt cold almost all the time. As if she would never be warm again.

Intellectually she knew that couldn't be true. She knew this feeling—a chill even in upper-90s weather—was all a product of her mind, her psyche. Her body wasn't really cold. She didn't have some rare disease or unknown illness. It was all inside her head. She'd taken her temperature to make sure.

It had been completely normal.

Nothing was wrong with her physically. She'd double-checked with her doctor. Gone in for a physical. "A couple-years-late, quarter-of-a-century checkup," she'd told him, not wanting to bring up the fact that she had the heater running at her house even though winter had long since passed.

Ironically the doctor had not only declared her completely healthy, but had congratulated her on being more grounded and wise than many people her age who tended to avoid physicals until something was wrong.

Sherry didn't avoid physicals. But it seemed that her mind was doing its best to avoid reality.

She pulled her shirt around her more tightly. It wasn't just the cold. She also couldn't stand the thought of being exposed, of sitting out here with no cover. As if the clothing she wore would somehow keep her insides from fragmenting into a million pieces and flying away.

Icy and *fragmented*. Two words she would never have used to describe herself a year ago now fit her perfectly. She had seen too much, been close to too many people with shattered lives. Had worked for too long without a break, without giving herself a chance to recharge. To heal.

Now her mind was evidently taking over that duty for Sherry. She was getting a break from her work whether she wanted it or not.

Because if she thought the cold was bad on normal occasions, it was downright frigid every time she tried to pick up a pencil and sketch pad.

They both sat beside her under the umbrella on their own towel. She was further from picking them up than she was from stripping down to just her bathing suit and frolicking in the sun.

She missed drawing. Creating the pictures of what she saw in her head. And more recently, creating the pictures other people saw in their heads.

Unfortunately those had turned out to be hideous monsters. A shiver rushed through her and she brought her knees up to her chest, wrapping her arms around them and rocking herself slightly back and forth.

At one time she had drawn every day, all the time. Growing up, she'd drawn or painted or colored on anything she could get her hands on: notebook paper, computer paper, the insides of book covers.

As she'd gotten older and realized there were *actual art supplies* she could buy, she'd rarely been without a sketch pad. Drawing was a part of her. All her friends had learned that Sherry would always be drawing—and usually drawing the people around her—no matter what else was going on. They'd accepted her; had learned that just because there was a pencil flying in her hand and her nose was in her sketchbook didn't mean she was ignoring them.

Her passion had driven her parents—both successful business owners, neither of them with any artistic ability or inclination—a little nuts. Both of them had small companies that could be handed down to Sherry if she would just do the smart thing: go to college and get a business degree. Or even better, a double major in business and something equally useful such as marketing or finance.

Sherry had double-majored, but in what *she* had found interesting: art and psychology. The psychology mostly because understanding what was going on inside the human mind made for more compelling drawings.

For the four years right after college Sherry had found moderate success in the art world. She wasn't ever going to be rich, but she at least didn't have to wait tables.

Then two years ago she'd stumbled onto what some people in law enforcement had termed her "obvious calling."

Forensic art.

Sherry could admit it was the perfect blend of her natural artistic gifting and what she'd learned with her psychology degree. Once the FBI had learned that she was so good at it, she'd worked consistently—really beyond full-time—for them for the past two years. But if she had known the cost would be her love and passion for drawing, she had to wonder if she would ever have gotten involved with the FBI in the first place.

That seemed like such a selfish statement. She didn't like to think that she would give up the breakthroughs she'd made in cases, the criminals she'd had a part in helping apprehend, just because it made her not want to draw anymore.

But she hadn't even so much as picked up drawing materials for pleasure in more than six months. For the past five months, she'd drawn what she'd needed to for cases, although it had been difficult.

Then last month, after a particularly brutal case, the cold had started. She'd barely made it through her last two cases after that. Her boss at the FBI was glad Sherry was taking a couple of weeks off. It would allow her to "recover and come back fully recharged and ready to do what she did best—listen to a victim, get the picture in her mind and draw it so law-enforcement officers could put another bad guy away."

That was a direct quote. And pretty much the farthest from reality than Sherry had ever felt.

How could she be ready to jump back into forensic art when, even now on vacation, with the vast beauty of the Gulf in front of her fairly begging Sherry to attempt to capture its beauty on paper, she couldn't even pick up a pencil?

All she could do was keep from shivering and flying apart.

It was the third day of her two-week vacation in Corpus Christi. She'd actually made it outside today rather than just looking at the water from her house on the beach, one her parents owned but never used. So maybe she should cut herself a little slack.

She had made it to the beach today. That was enough. Tomorrow she would go a little further. Would actually pull out her sketch pad and draw *something*, even if it resembled a kindergartener's stick figure. And even if she had to put a coat on to do it.

Maybe the day after that she'd actually take off her polar tundra gear and dip her feet in the Gulf. One thing Sherry had learned from working over and over with traumatized people was that you just had to take it a little bit at a time. It was okay to expect that same slow progress from herself.

In a few minutes she'd be driving into downtown Corpus Christi to pick up her friend Caroline. They'd gone to college in Dallas at the same time and had taken a few psychology classes together and then kept in touch. Caroline was a paramedic here in the city.

Sherry would at least slip on a short-sleeved blouse and skirt before meeting her friend. Caroline was already concerned about her. She would be even more worried if Sherry showed up dressed as she was now, particularly in this heat. Sherry hadn't shared what was going on with her—she hadn't wanted to worry her friend. But even without talking about it, she knew Caroline was concerned.

Dinner and margaritas on the back patio of Pier 99, a pier turned restaurant on North Beach, with a good friend and no pressures sounded perfect to Sherry.

No trauma. No stress. No need to force herself to draw. Just margaritas.

JON HATTON HAD a barbecue brisket sandwich—he wasn't ashamed to admit that he'd developed an addiction to the Texas staple in his week of being here—almost up to his mouth when he received the brief text. Another rape victim. Memorial.

Even though it broke part of his heart, he dropped his half-eaten sandwich and stood.

Jon threw down a twenty, more than enough to pay for his meal at the diner plus leave the waitress a hefty tip, and was running out the door less than fifteen seconds after he received the text.

CHRISTUS Spohn Hospital Corpus Christi— Memorial for short—was right smack in the middle of downtown. Jon knew where Memorial was. But not because of any information local law enforcement had provided him, only because of the maps he had studied.

Corpus Christi PD was pretty pissed that Jon, a member of Omega Sector: Critical Response Division, was even here. They had made it clear they didn't find his skills as a behavioral analyst and expertise in crisis management needed or welcomed.

That was just too damn bad because they very definitely had a crisis on their hands. Corpus Christi had a serial rapist on the loose.

Five rapes in just over eight weeks. Actually six now, if the current woman in the hospital was also a victim. The local police, as probably any police force of a city this size, didn't have the resources to deal with this type of situation.

People were in a panic and no breaks had been made on the case.

Corpus Christi PD had wanted to handle the situation themselves. But once the story made national news, that option was no longer available.

Omega had been called in and Jon, highly experienced with situations where multiple skills would be necessary—profiling, crime and linkage analysis, investigative suggestions, multiagency coordination—had been sent.

Jon was good at seeing the overall big picture, at catching details other people sometimes missed. At taking all the individual pieces involved in a case of this magnitude and putting them together so that the whole was more than the sum of the parts.

He was also a pilot, an excellent sharpshooter and could kill a man a dozen different ways with his bare hands. But that probably wasn't in his official dossier.

No matter what list of credentials Omega had provided for Jon's arrival to help with this case, it hadn't made any difference with the locals. Every piece of information was only reluctantly shared. Jon was the last person notified for any possible lead.

But call him Rhett Butler because, frankly, Jon didn't give a damn. He wasn't in Corpus Christi to sit around holding hands and singing "Kumbaya." He was here to stop a predator from victimizing more women.

A particularly smart predator who was too clever to leave behind any evidence so far.

So it wasn't as if the Christi locals could be accused of not doing their jobs properly. Jon hadn't been able to make as much as a single crack in the case himself, despite the time he'd spent in his week here interviewing victims and studying patterns.

It was a frustrating feeling when all he could do was wait for the bad guy to strike again and hope for a mistake. Not a feeling Jon was used to or that sat well with him.

This was the first victim that had been reported since Jon had arrived in town. He planned to make sure there wasn't a next, regardless of how cooperative the Corpus Christi PD was. Or wasn't.

The text notifying him of the victim hadn't come from a member of the police department. Oh, Jon had no doubt they would eventually get around to notifying him of the victim's existence. After all, none of them wanted to be accused of deliberately keeping info from him. But God only knew when that would actually be.

The text had come from Caroline Gill, a paramedic. Jon had met and befriended her and her partner, Michael Dutton, earlier in the week when he'd interviewed them about victim number two, whom they'd also transported a few weeks ago.

Dutton and Gill weren't threatened by Jon's presence here. They had talked openly with him about what they knew, what they'd heard. Jon had even asked them their theories about the case, since they had been the first people on one of the crime scenes.

Perhaps the paramedics' opinions wouldn't amount to anything useful whatsoever. But Jon had been doing this job for Omega Sector long enough to know that a break in a case could often come from unusual sources.

At the very least, his willingness to listen to them had gotten him the text that had him now driving through the city as fast as he safely could.

Jon parked at the closest nonemergency spot he could find at Memorial and jogged to the sliding glass of the emergency entrance door, ignoring the muggy heat that was so unlike the weather in his home state of Colorado. He pulled out his credentials to show the nurse at the front desk, explaining who he was here to see. He was glad when he saw Sara Beth Carreker, the head nurse who had worked in Emergency for years, walk up. Jon had talked to her a few days ago, also, since all the victims had been brought to Memorial's Emergency Trauma Center.

Nurse Carreker's nod was brisk. "I'll show you back there myself. The patient has been moved into one of the private trauma care rooms." Her lips pinched together.

"I take it that's a bad sign?"

The nurse glanced at him as they walked down the hall. "Medically, it's pretty neutral. Just my opinion, of course. You'll have to ask the doctor for a professional statement." The older woman's eyes argued that she had seen more and probably knew more than a lot of the young doctors around here.

"So, physically she'll recover. That's not why she's in the room." Jon's words weren't questions.

"Yes." Nurse Carreker nodded as they turned a corner. "Emotionally that woman needs as much privacy as she can get."

"Anything you can tell me about her?"

"Young. A local. African-American this time, so that's a little different. But the same type of bruising and craniofacial trauma."

A black female. Jon's jaw clenched. The demographic pattern of the women who had been attacked was widely varied, almost unheard of in a serial rapist. It was one of the reasons Corpus Christi PD had resisted asking for any federal help. Since serial rapists usually had a set type of woman they attacked, the department hadn't thought the perpetrator was just one person.

Nurse Carreker stopped halfway down the hall. "Agent Hatton, y'all try to remember that this isn't a case to that woman. Her whole world has just been destroyed."

Y'all? Just because Jon didn't use the word didn't mean he didn't know what it meant. How many people were here besides him? "Okay, thank you."

The nurse patted him on the arm and left. Jon turned back toward the victim's room. At least half a dozen of Corpus Christi's finest were standing around outside the victim's door. They alternated between glaring at and completely ignoring him as he approached.

Damn, this was going to be a long afternoon.

Chapter Two

Jon noticed that Zane Wales, the detective he'd been working most closely with—*closely* being a very relative term—was busy cross-referencing something on his smartphone with a file in his hands. The younger man made it a point not to make eye contact. Wales should've been the one who had called or texted Jon, not the paramedic.

Jon tamped down his frustration. This wasn't the time or place to get into it with Wales again. Especially because he knew the captain at the local police department all but applauded Wales's attitude. He encouraged any and all negative attitudes toward Jon.

"Hatton," Wales said neutrally in greeting. The man actually wore a cowboy hat all the time. Since they were in Texas that shouldn't surprise Jon, but it was still a little unsettling.

"Wales." Jon raised an eyebrow, but didn't say anything further.

"Doctor's with the victim, so no one can go

in yet." Wales put himself between the door and Jon as if Jon were going to barge his way in. Jon barely restrained himself from rolling his eyes.

He looked over at the uniformed officers milling around, half a dozen of them, all male. They all wanted to be here, be somewhere nearby so they could help if needed. While Jon appreciated the gesture, they had to leave.

He turned back to Wales. "A little crowded out here, don't you think, for a woman who's just been brutally attacked?"

Wales looked a little surprised that Jon had said something reasonable. Probably had expected him to pick a fight about not being notified.

"Actually, I agree," Wales said. "The last thing that woman is going to want or need is a bunch of people—men especially, probably—out here hanging around."

The detective's statement reassured Jon on multiple levels. First, he had already been aware of the problem before Jon even pointed it out and would've handled it himself soon, hopefully. Second, Wales might not like him or the fact that he had been assigned to the case, but at least he wasn't going to do something potentially case-damaging such as keep a bunch of unnecessary people there just to spite Jon. The victim was Wales's priority.

So cowboy hat notwithstanding—the jury was

definitely still out on that—the young detective had just proved himself to be at least competent and focused.

Jon backed out of the way as Wales went to talk to the uniformed officers and dismiss them. He could hear him reassure the men that they personally would be the first ones called if anything could be done for the victim or if any further help was needed. He was glad to see Wales wasn't a jerk in general.

Just with him, evidently.

After the uniforms left, Wales made his way over to Jon. Both knew it could be some time before they were able to talk to the victim, depending on the extent of the physical and emotional trauma. But sooner was definitely better, while everything was, unfortunately, still fresh in the victim's mind.

They'd have to wait until the doctor came out to give them more information.

"Do we know anything about the victim?" Jon gave it about a fifty-fifty chance that the detective would be forthcoming with information.

Wales hesitated but then responded.

"Vic's name is Jasmine Houze. She's twenty-seven, not married, lives on Mustang Island, which is out near the beach. Works for Flint Hill Resources, an oil company."

Corpus Christi, in Jon's opinion, was a city with an identity crisis: part touristy beach town, part oil/shipping industry. Both businesses seemed to vie for what the city would be known for. There were lovely beaches, but if you wandered too far from them you were right in the middle of oil industry with their buildings and warehouses and machinery. So you had all types of people in the city's makeup.

"Nurse said there was similar craniofacial trauma?" Jon asked.

"I haven't seen her yet or any medical records to confirm," Zane Wales responded. "But, yeah, I understand that's the case."

The extent of the woman's wounds would determine a lot, such as how soon they could question her and to what degree she would be able to coherently remember facts.

It was a full hour later before the doctor, a female, and two female nurses came out. The doctor closed the door behind her in a way that suggested no one would be entering soon.

"Gentlemen," the doctor said in greeting.

"How is she, Dr. Rosemont?" Wales asked. "Is it possible for us to speak with her?"

Jon stayed a half step back. It was better for local detectives to take the lead in these types of cases, he knew from experience. He would only jump in if necessary.

Although the nurses left to complete their other duties, the doctor positioned herself even more solidly in front of the door.

"As I'm sure you can imagine, Ms. Houze is in a delicate state right now, both physically and emotionally." The doctor crossed her arms over her chest.

Jon was glad to see Wales nodding, taking seriously what the doctor was saying. It was important to talk to Ms. Houze, but it was also important to remember that this was the worst day of her entire life.

"We understand," Wales said. "And we want to be sensitive to the situation. But talking to her soon is important, if medically possible."

"Ms. Houze has significant bruising to her face and jaw. The rapist struck her a half-dozen times in rapid succession to stun her. She'll have no permanent damage from those blows, but both her eyes are currently swollen shut."

That was undoubtedly what the attacker had intended, so the victim wouldn't be able to identify him. Jon grimaced. The same thing had happened in the other cases. As a matter of fact, the facial abuse was what had helped alert them to the fact that this was the work of a single man.

"Do you think she'll be willing to talk with us?" Wales asked her.

"I definitely don't think she's interested in surrounding herself with men right now, so only one of you, and that may not work at all." Dr. Rosemont shrugged.

"Then I'll be handling that, boys." The drawl came from behind them.

Jon turned the find the last person he would send into a room with a woman who had been victimized. Senior detective Frank Spangler.

Unlike Wales, who might not like Jon personally, but at least showed promise as a detective, Frank Spangler was the epitome of everything that could be considered bad about law enforcement.

The man had been wearing a badge for too long. He had lost touch with what was most important about his career: namely that he was supposed to serve the people. Spangler was smug and crass and definitely not the person best suited to question a woman who'd just been viciously attacked.

Unfortunately, Detective Spangler was not only the ranking detective, but he was also the Nueces County forensic artist. The *only* one. Jon had already checked.

Jon had seen Spangler's composite drawings for other cases and had to admit the man had some skill with a pencil. But for the current case, none of the victims had seen the rapist's face. They'd all been hit so hard, so quickly, that they'd been completely disoriented and unable to get a clear view before their attacker had pushed them down. So even if Spangler had some drawing talent, gathering any usable intel from the victims hadn't been possible.

But maybe Ms. Houze was different. They had to try.

Dr. Rosemont nodded at the older detective. "That's fine. But under no circumstances are you all to barge in on her at once. My word is law around here, gentlemen. Remember that. Door open at all times and if Ms. Houze says she's had enough, you're to leave immediately."

Jon and Zane both nodded at the doctor. Frank Spangler just gave her a patronizing smile. Her lips pursed.

"I'll check with her and be right out." The doctor knocked softly on the door and made her way inside.

Caroline Gill, the paramedic who had sent Jon the text alerting him of the new victim, joined them in the hallway.

"Hi, Jon. Hey, Zane," Caroline said. She smiled at Jon. But her eyes, he realized, were only for Zane. The detective, on the other hand, didn't really seem to notice the pretty paramedic.

He barely glanced at her from where he was looking over a file in his hand. "Hey, Caroline."

"I'm just getting off work and waiting on my ride."

"Where's your car?" Jon asked her since Zane seemed oblivious that Caroline was here to see him.

"A friend from college is in town and is going to pick me up in a few minutes so we can go to dinner. She dropped me off for my shift this morning so I wouldn't have to find parking."

Wales nodded without even looking up from his file. Caroline's face was a little crestfallen at his behavior.

"Hey, thanks for the text," Jon said to her to change the subject.

Zane looked up sharply at that. He had probably wondered how Jon had gotten here so fast. Well, now he knew.

"Really?" Zane asked Caroline.

Caroline turned toward him and put her hands on her hips. "You know for a detective, Zane Wales, sometimes you're pretty obtuse. So, yeah, *really.*"

Jon swallowed his chuckle.

Frank Spangler cleared his throat and began sorting through items in his briefcase, pulling out some drawing materials. "I doubt this victim will have kept her wits about her any more than any of the others. But here's to hoping."

Jon grimaced and heard Caroline's gasp. Zane's level of obtuse was nothing compared to Frank Spangler's.

"You sure that's the right attitude to go in there with?" Jon asked Spangler. "I'm pretty sure being told she should've kept her wits about her as she was being attacked is not the best way to start an interview."

"Look, I was doing this job before you were

in training pants." Spangler sneered at Jon. "I'm not going to say that to *her*, of course. You just stay out and let me work."

It didn't matter if Spangler was going to say it or not. He *thought* it. That was bad enough.

But unless the older man did something illegal or to outright jeopardize the case, there wasn't anything Jon could do. Corpus Christi had been forced to allow him here and give him access to all the information, but it was still their case. From experience, Jon knew that allowing them to handle as much as possible was best in the long run for both the department and the community.

But listening to Spangler's idiocy still wasn't easy. Caroline looked as though she was about to let Spangler have it when the doctor came out the door again.

"Ms. Houze has agreed to see you—*one* of you, like I said. I have suggested she limit the time you're in there to fifteen minutes. She has family on their way. She needs them right now."

"Yeah, well, I would think she would want us to catch the person who did this," Spangler muttered.

"Fifteen minutes, Detective. Tops. I'll be back then." Dr. Rosemont made her way down the hall.

The older officer wasted no time going in, sketch pad and pencil in hand.

"That man is a Grade-A jerk," Caroline snapped.

Jon couldn't agree more.

Zane didn't even disagree. "Fortunately he's only a year from retiring. Plus he's pretty good with composite drawing." The detective shrugged.

They could hear Spangler inside talking to the victim. He'd at least started the conversation by offering appropriate condolences for what had happened. Jon was distracted from listening by the woman who had walked silently down the hall and was now speaking to Caroline.

Blond hair with gentle waves that fell past her shoulders. Slender—almost too slender. A little taller than average height, maybe five foot eight in her knee-length skirt and brown cowboy boots. As with cowboy hats, Jon had never been one for boots, but he could already feel his opinion changing about that. This woman's brown, well-worn ones made it difficult for him to tear his attention from her legs.

Her legs were gorgeous. *She* was gorgeous.

This must be the friend from college the paramedic had mentioned. Caroline walked over with her to where he and Zane were standing.

"Zane, Jon, this is my friend Sherry Mitchell. She's visiting Corpus Christi for a couple of weeks," Caroline told them.

Jon shook Sherry's hand and immediately noticed she was distracted. Her eyes kept darting to the room where Spangler was talking to the victim.

Maybe because it was starting to get a little louder in there.

"Look, I'm your best bet in us apprehending the man who raped you. Do you really want to rest more than you want to catch this guy?" Spangler's voice could be heard clearly.

All the color seemed to seep out of Sherry's face.

"Look, don't cry, for heaven's sake." Spangler continued, his distaste obvious. "I'm a forensic artist. Just tell me what you saw."

"I didn't see anything." Jasmine Houze's voice was soft, slurred, probably from the swelling of her face. "I didn't see him. He hit me and then... and then... I'm sorry." Her crying became louder.

"Nothing?" Spangler demanded. "Nothing at all? Do you not want to catch him? Is that it?"

"Oh, my God," Sherry whispered.

"I'm going in there," Jon said to Zane. "I don't care if Spangler is the ranking officer or not. This has to stop."

"I'm right behind you," Zane agreed.

"No." It was Sherry who spoke. "That woman does not need more men barging in on her and fighting."

Caroline nodded. "She's right. I'll go in. I, at least, have already met her, since Michael and

I brought her in this morning. You guys go get the doctor."

"I'm going with you," Zane said to Caroline. "You know Spangler won't listen to you. He won't listen to Hatton, either."

"Well, for God's sake, shut him up," Jon said. "I'm going to get the doctor."

Sherry had just backed away against the wall. Jon didn't blame her. He'd stay out of this mess, too, if he was her. But she had lost all color and was shivering.

"Are you okay?" he asked, touching her gently on the upper arm.

She nodded without answering, her eyes still drawn toward the victim's room.

Caroline and Zane had already entered. Jon could hear Caroline talking softly to the woman.

Jon looked at Sherry again. "Are you sure you're okay?" He didn't want her to collapse.

"I'm fine," she said. It looked as though her teeth were about to start chattering, but he knew that couldn't be right; it wasn't nearly cold enough in here.

Sherry cocked her head toward the nurses' station. "Just go."

Jon took off running down the hallway to find Dr. Rosemont or Nurse Carreker. Either of them would help put an end to this without damaging Jasmine Houze's psyche further.

He found them both just moments later. Neither woman wasted time and the three of them were soon sprinting down the hallway toward the victim's room, Jon explaining as they ran.

The doctor and nurse, along with Caroline, distracted and comforted Ms. Houze as Jon and Zane both each grabbed one of Frank Spangler's arms.

"Wait, I'm not finished talking to her," Spangler all but screeched.

All three women surrounding the victim turned at the same time and said, "Yes. You are."

Fortunately, Spangler didn't put up a fight; he just walked out, huffing as he went. Jon immediately closed the door behind them.

"You better believe the captain's going to hear about this." Spangler's eyes glared at Jon as if he were personally responsible for him being kicked out of the victim's room. The older man then turned, gathered his things and left.

That was fine. Jon didn't care as long as Spangler wasn't allowed near Jasmine Houze or any of the victims again. And, yes, the police captain *would* hear about this. Jon glanced over at Zane, who just shrugged, shaking his head.

Caroline came out of the room, closing the door softly behind her. "They've given Jasmine a sedative. Her family should be here soon."

Jon looked over to where Sherry had been standing against the wall when he had last seen her. He wanted to talk to her more, to apologize for the craziness, to make sure she was all right.

And to ask her to dinner.

But she was gone.

Chapter Three

The next day Jon was ready to dig a hole and bury himself in it.

For one thing, it was one million degrees outside. He missed the Rocky Mountains of Colorado Springs where Omega Sector: Critical Response Division headquarters was located. He missed the crisp air, often cool even now in June, and the ability to go out and run first thing in the morning or even in the afternoons a lot of the time, and still be pretty comfortable.

Because this face-melting heat of Corpus Christi was probably going to kill him.

Not that he would be going out for a run anytime soon. Why run outside when he could just run in circles inside Corpus Christi Police Department, accomplishing nothing?

He was sitting in Captain Harris's office, along with Zane Wales and Frank Spangler. Spangler was categorically dismissing the complaints that had been called in against him by Jasmine

Houze's doctor. He actually called both the victim and Dr. Rosemont "irrational."

Wales had remained silent, refusing to either confirm or deny what had happened in the hospital room.

And while Jon appreciated that the younger man probably didn't want to get Frank Spangler in trouble just before his retirement, Zane's silence was not helping the case. If the Corpus Christi PD wasn't careful, they were going to lose control of the case entirely. One phone call from Jon and this case would be under federal jurisdiction rather than local.

That was a last-resort option and Jon didn't want to do that if he didn't have to. But he wouldn't hesitate if something like that happened again. He'd already made that clear to Captain Harris privately.

"We're going to need another forensic artist," Jon said to the other men.

"Well, that's too bad, since I'm the only one currently licensed in the county. And in our county only people licensed in forensic art are allowed to talk to witnesses or victims in an official capacity." Spangler sat back, secure in his own importance.

"My resources aren't limited to your county, Spangler," Jon said. "And believe me, I would go in there with a paper and pencil myself before I would let you further traumatize another woman like yesterday."

Spangler let out a loud huff. "You see there, Captain? This sort of unfriendly attitude is what we have to deal with all the time from Agent Hatton, all but impeding our investigation—"

Jon resisted the urge to jump out of his chair. Barely. "Are you kidding me? You just had a complaint filed against you from one of the top trauma doctors in the state. And you want to say I'm impeding the investigation?"

"Boys, enough," Captain Harris interrupted in his Texan drawl. "Hatton, please use your federal resources to find another forensic artist."

The captain's contempt for anything federal was evident by the way he said the word with a sneer.

"Fine." Jon's teeth were clenched, but he got the single syllable out.

"Now, if you don't mind, Agent Hatton, I'd like to talk to Detective Spangler alone. Sort through some things."

Somehow Jon didn't think that the "sorting" would involve any sort of reprimand whatsoever. Spangler's snigger and mock salute to Jon suggested the older man knew it, too.

Jon nodded, got up and left. He was afraid if he stayed he would end up punching Spangler, a man who was at least twenty-five years older than Jon's thirty-one. Jon's mom had taught him better than that.

Although Jon wasn't entirely sure his mother wouldn't have punched Frank Spangler herself if she'd been around yesterday.

He made his way over to the desk the department had given him in the darkest, stalest corner of the old brick building. It was right next to the copy machine and cleaning supplies, so it pretty much ensured that Jon dealt with a constant flow of interruptions and had a headache from the chemicals.

Still, it was better than being outside where his shoes would probably melt into the sidewalk. And this was nothing compared to August's heat evidently. That made Jon, a Cincinnati boy at heart, make a mental note to never travel this far south during that month if he could possibly help it.

He sat in his desk chair and spun it around so his back was to the rest of the desks, giving him at least a semblance of privacy. The copy machine wasn't so loud that way, either. He speed-dialed the direct office line for his boss, Steve Drackett, at Omega.

"You bought a cowboy hat yet?" Steve asked by way of greeting.

Jon chuckled slightly. "No. But I'm considering just killing someone on this force and taking his."

"That bad, huh?"

"To say they don't want me here would be a gross understatement. Don't mess with Texas and all that." Jon sighed. "We've got a new victim as of yesterday."

"I heard."

Jon wasn't surprised his boss already knew about Jasmine Houze. Steve tended to know a lot of things about a lot of things.

"I haven't talked to her yet. There was a whole brouhaha at the hospital with one of the senior-ranking detectives. Guy doesn't have bedside manner worth spit and traumatized the poor victim even more than she already was."

"Guy sounds like a problem?" his boss asked.

"Yeah, but he's a year out from retirement, so nobody's going to do anything about him unless he really screws things up."

"You need me to send in help?"

Jon leaned back farther in his chair. "No, I can handle it. I'm not here to make friends. But I guess I should tell you that I gave the police captain final notice about federal takeover." Jon explained exactly what had happened with Frank Spangler and the complaint.

"Well, I've got your back. You say the word and Omega will completely take over. I can have more agents down there in four or five hours." Steve chuckled. "I could have them there in less if you were here to fly them."

Jon smiled at that. "Thanks. It's better for everyone around here if the locals handle it. Good for morale and community relations. If they can't get it together, I'll let you know."

"Any actual progress?" Steve asked.

"Nothing, Steve. That's what kills me. I can't even blame it on Corpus Christi PD. I may not like any of them personally, but they're not inept. This guy is smart. A planner."

"You got a profile worked out on him yet?"

Jon spun his chair around so that he was facing the rest of the desks in the station. The activity and blur of noise actually helped him think.

"He's educated, or at least smart enough to know not to leave any DNA behind. Not even skin cells. These rapes are definitely acts of dominance, not rage. The perpetrator is in complete control of his emotions."

"I thought reports said the women had been beaten?" Drackett cut in. "That's not anger-based?"

"I don't think so," Jon replied, leaning back farther in his chair. "He only hits them enough to stun them. None of the women has had any broken or fractured noses or cheekbones. If the beatings were out of anger, the facial trauma would've been much greater. It was a deliberate move to keep them from being able to see and identify him."

It was great to let his thought process have

free rein with someone who wasn't throwing unnecessary questions or playing devil's advocate just to try to stump him. That was how his conversations with the local detectives had gone over the past week: a constant battle to one-up him.

"Nothing else about this guy is consistent but the craniofacial trauma. His victims are of varied race and age. The times of the attack are all over the place. The locations of the attacks are varied, also—most have been at the victims' homes, but one was at a hotel."

"And no evidence found at any of the scenes?"

"Nothing usable. None of the women got a clean punch or scratch." A single scratch from any of them would've given them trace DNA under their nails, but none of them had been able to do any damage to their attacker. "Each time, as soon as they opened the door, he hit them hard and fast, dazing them and causing swelling in both eyes, effectively blinding them."

He heard Steve's muttered curse. It echoed exactly how Jon felt.

"If that's the case, I'm sure none of the victims has been able to provide any sort of identifying marks or features," Steve said.

Jon grimaced. "No, not at all. But I have to say, if Frank Spangler has been the only forensic artist available to talk to the victims, maybe more information can be gathered from them, if his actions yesterday are anything to go by."

"Were there other complaints lodged against him?"

"No, but even if he wasn't as combative with the other women as he was yesterday, he still wasn't going to inspire any confidence in the victims. We need someone else, Steve."

"Omega has a few on retainer, but none in Texas. Let me make some calls and see what I can find out."

"Okay, I'm heading over to the crime scene. I'm not expecting much, but at least I'll be able to see this one firsthand rather than through pictures like the others," Jon said.

"Good luck. I'll send you the info when I find someone."

Jon ended the call. Steve would find another forensic artist if there was one around to be had. If not, he'd work his magic and find someone who *wasn't* around. Steve always made sure his agents had what they needed. And God knew Jon needed a better artist than Frank Spangler.

He saw Detective Wales making his way over, cowboy hat still firmly on his head. "You ready to go check out the crime scene?"

Jon lifted a single eyebrow. "We're going together?"

The younger man rolled his eyes. "I'm not asking you out on a date, Hatton. Captain just said

Spangler probably needed to stay away from anything having to do with Jasmine Houze, so I thought we would go together since we're both headed out there anyway."

Maybe Wales was just trying to make up for not saying anything to the captain about Spangler's true behavior. Whatever it was, Jon would take the peace flag being offered to him.

The drive from the station to the victim's house was mostly made in silence except for the country-western music coming from the radio of Wales's SUV. Honestly it wasn't half-bad. Maybe Jon should give the genre more of a chance.

Jasmine Houze's home was close enough to the beach to be desirable, but not so close that the price would be in the stratosphere. She was probably a good fifteen-minute walk from the water itself. The neighborhood looked to be in decent shape, certainly not a place where you were afraid to open your own door in the middle of the day.

At least that was what everyone had assumed until yesterday. Jon would damn well bet there was a whole new set of chains and bolts that had been installed on neighboring doors in the past twenty-four hours.

The houses were just far enough apart from each other to afford some privacy. The victim's was one of the four on the street that had large shrubbery in the front yard. Better for privacy.

Unfortunately it made the attack more private, also.

The three front steps leading up to the house had been taped off. Jon could see that the crime lab had already been here: print dust lay all along the railing leading up to the house and the door frame. If this was anything like the other scenes, it would soon be evident that the rapist had worn gloves.

Although Jon and Zane looked around, inside the house didn't yield any more results than outside. They would wait for results from the crime lab, but Jon wasn't holding his breath.

Their next two hours were spent talking to neighbors. Uniformed officers had already taken preliminary statements, but follow-ups were always necessary. Just as with the porch and the house, they discovered nothing. No one had heard anything out of the ordinary yesterday. No one had seen anyone unusual or suspicious walking or driving around lately. No strange cars. Nothing out of place.

Jon was frustrated, but he wasn't surprised.

"I read your preliminary behavioral analysis of the perp," Zane said as they stepped out into the heat after talking to the last neighbor.

He had read Jon's report? That did surprise him. He'd expected it to end up in the electronic trash bin on Wales's computer. He was sure that was where it had ended up in most everyone else's.

"Did you agree with the analysis?" Jon asked.

Zane shrugged and adjusted his hat to settle more fully on his head. "I don't disagree with any of it. Like you said, our guy is smart, focused, patient. The other rape cases I've dealt with haven't been that way. It's been more about rage and dominance."

Jon nodded. "Yeah, most rapists have those characteristics. And maybe our guy does, too, and has just figured out how to hide it."

The detective pondered that for a moment. "I guess what doesn't sit right with me is the fact that he's so smart we're having to sit around and wait for him to strike in order to gather more info."

Jon nodded. He had thought almost the exact same thing yesterday. His eyes tightened behind the sunglasses protecting him from the blazing sun. They were waiting for this guy to make a mistake. And that was not a position Jon wanted to be in.

They were almost back at the station when Jon got the text from Steve Drackett.

Found you a forensic artist. Exceptional recommendations from FBI in Houston. Full file sent.

"Looks like Omega found us another forensic artist," Jon said to Zane. "Maybe this will get us somewhere."

Everyone, especially Spangler, was glaring at Zane upon their entrance into the station. Evidently no one was thrilled with the younger detective's choice to spend time with Jon. Zane shrugged in half apology and left Jon, heading in a different direction.

Jon sighed. So much for making headway with the locals. But as he'd told Steve, he wasn't here to make friends. He grabbed a Coke—not a soda, pop or cola; they were *all* called *Coke* here, he'd been told—and went to his desk, the smell of cleaning agents permeating the air.

He was hot, he was frustrated and he was getting tired of the literal and figurative toxic environment surrounding him.

Most of all, Jon was frustrated that they couldn't get ahead of this bastard.

He sat down to pull up the file on the computer the department had given him—surprisingly one that worked—so he could print the info Steve had sent him on the forensic artist right away.

He took a sip of his soda then almost spewed it out.

Because, damn, if he didn't find the familiar features of Sherry Mitchell staring back at him.

Chapter Four

Sherry was just as lovely in her photo as she had been in real life. It was just a head shot, so unfortunately those legs he'd seen yesterday in the hospital weren't in it, but her long blond hair and clear blue eyes were.

Although Jon could appreciate her attractiveness, he was damn well ticked off at the woman.

How could she have stood there in the hallway yesterday and let Frank Spangler interview the victim? Not say a word about her profession?

And evidently she was stellar at it. If this file was anything to go by, Sherry Mitchell was considered by her supervisor at the FBI to be one of the best forensic artists in Texas, if not the entire Southwest. Her track record was impressive, and it seemed she had a particularly good case history with rape victims.

That just led Jon back to his original question: How could someone who obviously had a talent—having received numerous written commendations from some people pretty damn high up in the Bureau—just choose to do nothing yesterday?

Okay, she'd had dinner plans with Caroline. As trite as that sounded, Jon could actually understand that maybe Sherry hadn't wanted to break her reservation or whatever. But at the very least she could've offered to help at a later time, diffused the situation.

Not just stand there in the hallway shivering as though she'd never seen a trauma victim before.

Somewhere in his mind Jon knew he was being unfair, but he didn't care. He was damn well tired of every law-enforcement agent in the state having some sort of problem with him just because he was outside their don't-mess-with-Texas inner circle. Sherry Mitchell was the last straw.

He intended to let her know that.

The final part of Steve's message stated that although Sherry generally worked for the Houston Bureau field office, she was currently on vacation and her supervisor wasn't sure exactly where.

Jon knew, although not the exact place where she was staying.

But he knew how to get that info, too.

Jon grabbed his phone and called the number from the text he'd received yesterday notifying him of the new rape victim. He knew Caroline Gill would know where Sherry was staying.

"Hello?"

Caroline's voice sounded sleepy. Jon cringed. As a paramedic, Caroline probably worked odd hours. She might have been asleep.

"Hi, Caroline. It's Jon Hatton. I hope I didn't wake you."

"No, I'm fine. I have a shift in a couple of hours. Has something else happened?"

He could hear the concern in her voice. She was definitely wide-awake now. "No, no. Nothing new since Jasmine Houze. Actually, I was calling to ask you about your friend Sherry Mitchell."

"Oh. What about her?"

"I just thought I might stop by to talk to her, if you didn't mind?"

"You found out."

"Found out what?"

"About her being a forensic artist. She's on vacation, Jon. She needs a break."

Was Sherry really so selfish that she wouldn't take a day out of her precious vacation to help the Corpus Christi PD and a woman who had been through a hideous trauma?

"I just want to talk to her, Caroline. I don't want to push or cut into her time off. I'm sure she deserves it as much as anyone."

Jon tried to throw lightness into his tone. Caroline was concerned about her friend. It was an admirable trait even if he didn't see much about Sherry worth protecting if she was as shallow as her actions suggested. Obviously she was good at taking care of herself. She didn't need her perky friend to do it.

Caroline sighed. "She just seems so tired. Maybe that's not the right word, but I don't know exactly what is. She's just...she needs her vacation, Jon. Maybe you should leave her be."

For just a second Sherry's face—devoid of color, teeth almost chattering—flitted through his mind. Okay, yeah, maybe she was more tired or stressed or whatever than he was giving her credit for. But he had no intention of letting a forensic artist of her talent slip through his fingers when she was right in town and there was such a need.

Feeling bad, he shifted his tactics with Caroline.

"I do want to ask her professional opinion, but, really," he chuckled in self-mock, "I'm a little embarrassed to admit this because it's so middle-school-ish, but I was hoping to ask her out. Nothing serious or that would make her uncomfortable, just a meal or something."

That was the truth. Last night, before he'd known how self-centered Sherry obviously was, he had been quite interested in asking her out.

Now he was just interested in Sherry getting past her selfishness and doing her job as a forensic artist.

"Oh." Caroline hesitated, but then finally continued. "Well, that might be good for her. Just, like you said, keep it light." She gave him the address of Sherry's house on the beach. "If she doesn't like you, don't tell her I gave you her address."

"Thanks, Caroline. Maybe we could all go out together. Sherry and I, you and Zane."

Caroline guffawed. That was the only word for the sound that came over the phone. "Yeah, you work on that, Agent Hatton. Let me know how it goes."

The call ended. Jon had no idea what had or hadn't happened between Caroline and Zane Wales, but it was obviously complicated.

Jon had much more important things to worry about than romance between the detective and paramedic.

Right now he had a date of his own to get. And he didn't plan to take no as an answer.

SHERRY SAT IN almost the exact same place she had sat the day before, umbrella up, blocking her from most of the late-afternoon sun's rays.

She had her red bikini on again, but once again had clothes over it. This time at least it was lightweight linen capri pants rather than jeans. Much more appropriate for the beach. Her long-sleeved, button-down shirt was still a little conspicuous, but since it was unbuttoned, not too bad.

Sherry was determined not to let what she had

seen—or rather heard—at the hospital yesterday cause her to have a complete setback. To do that, she just had to completely shut the entire incident out of her mind.

It was hard. She had picked up the phone a half-dozen times last night to call Caroline and get the number of the handsome Detective Hatton and tell him that she would at least try to help. But every time she did she'd been racked with a cold so vicious she'd felt paralyzed. There was no way she was going to be of any use to anyone.

Even the cold wasn't as bad as reliving the scene of that poor woman crying as the jerk who called himself a police officer had tried to question her. That was heartbreaking. And knowing Sherry could've stepped in and taken over at any time, if she'd just been able to find the strength to do it, was agonizing.

So here she was, on the beach, putting it all out of her mind. It was her only option.

She had her pencil and sketch pad on her lap in the beach chair she sat in. She'd made random lines, nonsensical shapes to the rhythm of the gulf waves crashing a dozen yards away, but hadn't been able to force herself to do anything beyond that.

At least she wasn't shivering.

She was tempted to try to draw the face of Detective Hatton from last night, since it kept floating through her mind. She definitely remembered his exact features. Dark brown hair, cut short. Hazel eyes. Chiseled, clean-shaved jaw. Confidence permeated how he held himself; intelligence how he studied everyone around him to understand their motives and actions before he responded. The guardedness of his features probably wasn't let down very often.

Even without her talents as an artist she'd be able to remember him clearly. It wasn't a face one was likely to forget. And, Sherry could admit, it was the first time she had felt any heat by looking at a stranger in a long time. Months. Maybe longer.

Then that guy in the hospital room had started belittling the woman and the cold had swamped Sherry again. She'd been almost paralyzed with iciness. It was coming back again now, so she pushed all thoughts of yesterday, even of handsome Detective Hatton, out of her head. She kept her hand on the pencil, but nothing was coming from it.

A few moments later a larger shadow showed up next to her umbrella. Sherry looked over from the drawing she wasn't really drawing and saw casual brown oxfords coupled with dark khakis. Definitely not a bad style, but also not beach wear.

She shaded her face to allow her eyes to travel farther up and found a blue polo shirt neatly tucked into the pants and then the face of Detective Jon Hatton.

Speak of the devil.

"Aren't you a little overdressed for the beach?" he asked by way of greeting.

"No more so than you, Detective Hatton," Sherry responded. She felt at a distinct disadvantage being so far down near the ground with him towering over her. She couldn't see his face well because of the sun, but her brain was more than happy to fill in from memory whatever she couldn't physically see.

"Yeah, well, I'm not on vacation, as you so definitely are," he said.

The use of the word *vacation* seemed almost venomous. His entire frame radiated tension.

"Is that a problem?" she asked.

"Evidently not to you."

It didn't take a genius to see that the detective was mad. And his anger seemed to be directed at her.

"Is there something I can do for you, Detective Hatton? Some sort of problem?"

She could feel her fingers moving with the pencil over the paper, real shapes taking form this time, but she didn't pay it any mind. It wasn't the first time she'd drawn something without giving the paper her direct attention.

Her focus was on Hatton, who was still standing so she had to crane her neck to look up at him. No doubt it was on purpose. The man was too intelligent, too insightful, for it to be anything but a deliberate measure on his part.

It was kind of making her mad. And…hot.

Not a sexual hot, but a regular, healthy, over-heated hot because she was sitting on a Texas beach in the late-afternoon June sun in long pants and sleeves.

"Really?" he said. "You can't figure it out?"

God, it felt good not to be icy. Even if it took being around a jerk to do it. Evidently her attraction, or whatever she'd had for him in the first few moments she'd seen him yesterday, was way off base.

Sherry sat straighter in her chair. She wasn't just going to sit here and let him talk down to her, literally and figuratively. She got up from under her umbrella, tucking her pencil behind her ear, sketch pad down at her side.

At nearly five foot eight, Sherry was used to being pretty close to eye to eye with a lot of men, but not to Hatton. She hadn't realized how tall he really was. He had to be at least six foot three, because she *still* had to crane her neck to look up at him. Not something she was used to.

"What is it that you want, Detective Hatton?"

She studiously ignored how the blue in his shirt brought out the blue specks in his eyes, especially in the late-afternoon golden sun.

"What I want is to know why you didn't let me know about that." He pointed toward her waist.

She looked down at herself. Was he still talking about her clothes? "I get cold, okay? It's no crime to have on long sleeves at the beach."

"No." He closed the few feet between them and took the sketch pad that she held in her hand. "This."

He was studying the sketch pad. Sherry felt a flush creep across her cheeks. She didn't want to explain the random lines and doodles that covered her sketch pad. Didn't want to go into the whole story about her drawings or lack thereof. Whether he knew she was an artist or not, she didn't want to have to explain the lack of talent evident on that pad.

"Give it back to me." She reached for the pad, but he took a step backward so she couldn't reach it, still studying it.

"Why didn't you tell me about this yesterday?" He briefly shook the pad in his hand.

That she'd lost her ability to draw?

"Look, it's difficult to explain…"

"Really? What's so difficult about saying, 'I'm a forensic artist. Maybe I can help with the situation'?"

He turned the sketch pad around so what she had drawn was facing her. Sherry was already cringing, preparing to explain, until she got a glimpse of the drawing.

She had drawn Detective Hatton in almost perfect likeness.

Chapter Five

"I guess I'm flattered," Jon continued, holding the sketch pad.

Sherry just stood there, looking at the drawing. It wasn't her greatest work, by any means. Really it was just in the preliminary stages— rough lines and edges—but it was definitely him. It was the first work she'd done that wasn't just absolute crap in weeks.

She'd drawn it subconsciously. Not only was it not bad, but she hadn't gotten any chills when she did it. As a matter of fact, now that she was out from under the protection of the umbrella, she was downright hot. She took off her shirt and tied it around her waist. The sun on her back and shoulders felt wonderful.

But she wasn't quite sure exactly what conversation she was having with Jon Hatton.

"Why are you here?" she asked him.

"Why didn't you tell me you were a forensic artist yesterday at the hospital?"

"Believe it or not, I don't generally make those the first words out of my mouth when I'm talking to a complete stranger." She grabbed the sketch pad out of his hand.

"You saw what was going on with that woman yesterday, how poorly Frank Spangler was handling the interview for the composite drawing, and you did nothing. You ran away."

Sherry's mouth fell open before she closed it again. What was she supposed to say? It had been all she could do yesterday to just keep it together. The last thing on her mind had been to offer to help.

Yes, she had run away. She wouldn't have been any use to anyone anyway. She'd been shaking so hard she'd hardly been able to get her keys in the car door to unlock it.

But, damn, if she had to explain any of that to him. Jerk.

"Believe it or not, I don't walk around hospitals offering my services to everyone. I was there to pick up my friend. I just happened upon your situation accidentally."

She could tell right away that wasn't going to appease him.

"You were so busy with dinner plans that you couldn't help a woman who had just been through the most traumatic event of her life?"

"You know what, Detective Hatton? There was nothing I could've done yesterday. By the time you got in there and got *your man* out, the damage had already been done. That poor woman wasn't going to talk to anyone, no matter who the artist was."

"He's not my man," Hatton replied.

"Whatever. He's on your police force. Your team."

"No, I'm—"

Sherry held up a hand to cut him off. She wasn't really interested in discussing the idiot who'd further traumatized that woman. As far as she could tell, everyone employed in law enforcement in Corpus Christi was a jerk.

"Who told you I was a forensic artist? Caroline?" Sherry didn't think her friend would say anything, but maybe she had done so.

"No." He shook his head. "I knew we needed a different forensic artist since Spangler has been taken off the case, so I made a call."

"I'm glad to hear that Detective Spangler won't be doing any more damage."

"Me, too. He has no business being around any victims, as far as I'm concerned."

That made Sherry feel a little better. At least Hatton didn't defend Spangler. Sherry turned away and began loading up her beach stuff to take back to the house. She knew she wouldn't be sitting out here anymore today.

"I'm sorry you came all the way to the beach, Detective, if it wasn't to enjoy the sunshine. Because I can't help you. For the next two weeks I'm just a tourist not a forensic artist."

It sounded uncaring and cold even to her own ears. But what could she do about it? Except for the rough outline of Hatton's features—which really didn't count because, first, she hadn't been actually trying to draw him, her fingers had just taken over, and, second, there wasn't enough detail in it to be of any use for any police work anyway—she hadn't been able to draw a face in weeks.

She wasn't trying to be unfeeling; she just couldn't help Detective Hatton. She couldn't even help herself.

JON SWALLOWED HIS ANGER. *Just a tourist for the next two weeks?* That might possibly be the most selfish thing he'd ever heard. Sherry Mitchell might be drop-dead gorgeous in that red bikini top she was wearing, but it was obvious her beauty was only skin-deep.

If it even reached that far. Such a damn shame.

Jon had read in her file that both her parents owned separate successful businesses. Ms. Mitchell had obviously grown up spoiled, and those tendencies had remained when she became an adult.

Normally, Jon didn't mind spoiling the woman he was with. Enjoyed all the slightly crazy nuances that made women the mind-bogglingly lovely creatures that they were. He loved the mental acuity it required to discover what it was they really wanted.

But not in this case. Jon was pissed off at how the woman in front of him categorically refused to assist in a situation where she could really help. Now she was just folding up her chair and umbrella as if it were just another day at the beach. Which evidently it was to her.

No, what really made Jon mad was that he was *still* attracted to her despite her actions. He might think she was completely spoiled, but he knew that, given the chance, he would be kissing every inch of those shoulders and back she'd exposed when she tied that long-sleeved shirt around her waist.

Jon took a deep, cleansing breath. Neither focusing on Sherry's selfishness nor her beauty was getting him anywhere.

He needed to focus on how he could talk her into coming to the hospital and doing her magic as a forensic artist.

Jon had considerable people skills. That was one of the things that made him so good at his job at Omega. He kept a level head. He saw things others missed. He could read people, manipulate them when necessary.

It was time to put his distaste away and focus on getting Ms. Mitchell to do her job.

"It's 'agent.'"

She looked over her shoulder from where she was packing up her beach items. "I beg your pardon?"

"I'm Agent Hatton, not Detective Hatton."

"Agent as in FBI? You don't work for the Corpus Christi Police Department?"

So much for thinking she hadn't wanted to help him because he wasn't a local cop. She'd had no idea. That made him feel a little less hostile. "No, I don't work for the local PD or the Bureau. I work for Omega Sector in the Critical Response Division."

Sherry nodded. "Okay. I've heard a few people at the FBI field office talk about Omega. Sorry I called you 'detective.'"

"Why don't we just alleviate the problem altogether by you calling me Jon?" He gave her his most charming smile. The one that had always worked on his mom to get him out of trouble.

Sherry paused for just a moment, then nodded. "Okay, Jon. I'm Sherry. But you already knew that, I guess."

Jon kept his smile up. "I did."

"I guess that guy, Spangler, or whatever that moron's name is, really wasn't part of your team if you're not local PD, so please accept my apologies for that statement."

Jon shrugged. "No apologies necessary, but let me assure you that no one like Spangler would ever be on my team, much less be anywhere near a victim."

He could see her relax just the slightest bit and knew he was on the right track with what she needed to hear: that Spangler's actions were inexcusable.

No contest, as far as Jon was concerned.

He walked over and helped her lower the umbrella, which had reopened when she'd turned to talk to him. "Look, I'm sorry if I came across too strong a minute ago. But if you could take a few minutes out of your vacation to talk to Jasmine Houze, the victim, and see if there is anything you can help her remember, that would really be helpful."

Sherry looked at him and then quickly looked away. "Caroline told me none of the women had really gotten a look at the attacker. Is Ms. Houze any different?"

Jon grimaced. "Based on preliminary reports and what she told the doctors, no. It doesn't look like she got a good look at the rapist's face."

Sherry began stuffing all her beach items into a large bag. "Then you don't really need me. I can't help you."

Jon tamped his irritation down again. "All I'm asking is for you to try. You've got an excellent track record with cases like these, and you're a woman, which might make Ms. Houze more comfortable. Maybe she didn't see her attacker's face, but she might remember something. You're our best shot."

She looked as though she was going to say something but then stopped. Jon frowned as she took the long-sleeved shirt from around her waist and put it on as if she were chilly.

That would be fine if it wasn't ninety degrees outside right now. Jon was already wiping sweat from his face, and he was in a short-sleeved shirt. She was actually buttoning hers up.

"You okay?" he asked.

"Um, yeah. I just caught a little chill, that's all."

Okay, that was odd. She'd been shivering yesterday at the hospital, too. Interesting. An illness?

"Are you sick? Running a fever?"

"No. I just…" She shrugged one delicate shoulder not hidden under her long shirt. "I just get cold sometimes."

Jon wanted to pursue it further, but now was the time to push about the interview, while her defenses were weakened.

"Sherry, Ms. Houze needs you. There is no one else because of the licensing laws in Nueces County. If you don't try, Frank Spangler is the next best option."

Jon didn't say that there was no way that was going to happen, not with him here. But revealing that wouldn't help his argument with Sherry.

"I really can't help you." She huddled farther into her shirt.

"Can't or won't?"

"Does it make a difference?"

"I'm just asking you to try. An hour of your time? If you can't help after that, at least you tried. You didn't sit here doing nothing."

There was a long pause as she looked at him. She seemed to huddle down farther into her shirt.

"Okay, when?" she finally asked.

"Right now would be best." He didn't want to give her a chance to change her mind or to decide to make other plans.

She looked at him for another long, silent moment. "Fine, Agent Hatton. I will go and talk to the victim. I wouldn't expect anything to come of it, if I were you."

Jon nodded. "Just try. That's all I ask."

Chapter Six

This was not going to be pretty, in any sense of the word. Sherry dropped all her beach items in the screened-in porch attached to the back of the house. She would worry about the beach stuff later. Right now she needed to take a quick shower and change.

She was meeting Jon at the hospital. He'd offered her a ride, but after his pinball attitude toward her on the beach, Sherry knew driving herself was a better plan.

Once he saw she wasn't capable of drawing, she might be stranded in town if she rode with him.

He was pretty much a jerk. Handsome, with cheekbones so sharp you could cut yourself on them, but still a jerk. And if he thought she didn't know that he'd just *handled* her out there—pouring on his considerable charm and bright smile once the intimidation factor didn't work—then he was well mistaken. She knew she'd been managed; it had happened enough times with her parents for her to recognize the pattern.

The thing was, it wasn't that she didn't want to help out Jon or Jasmine Houze—what kind of unfeeling wretch would she be if that was the case?—but she didn't even think she was capable.

She would try. That was all she could do. All Agent Hatton had asked her to do. They'd see if he still felt that way when the pencil wouldn't move because of her shivering.

The thought brought on a bout of cold, despite the fact that she didn't have the air-conditioning running anywhere in the house. Sherry headed to the bathroom and stripped off her clothes, turning the water as hot as it could get without scalding her. She knew she wouldn't be able to stay in there long enough to really get warm—that would take so long, Jon would be in here managing her again—but at least it took a little of the edge off, warming the outside of her body if not the inside.

After her shower she dried her hair, which because of its thickness and length took a long time, but she knew better than to go out with it wet in a situation like this: if she got a chill, damp hair would just exacerbate it. She slipped on black jeans and a long-sleeved dark plum sweater and then pulled on her boots. After a touch of makeup—she wanted to look professional, for Jasmine Houze, not Jon Hatton—she grabbed her sketch pad and a set of pencils, and was out the door.

The drive to the hospital went faster than Sherry would've liked. She focused on a number of different things: the traffic, the scenery, the number of pickup trucks she could count, anything to keep her from thinking about what was coming up. She didn't want to be a shivering mess before she even set foot in the hospital.

Sherry had made it through her last two cases with the cold seeming to permeate her. She could make it through questioning one woman who they suspected hadn't seen anything. But, honestly, whether Jasmine had seen anything would be beside the point. Because either way, Sherry was going to have to walk with the poor woman through the worst day in her entire life.

She sighed as a chill rushed through her. Count pickups now. She'd be dealing with monsters soon enough.

As she found a parking place at the hospital, already having to grit her teeth to keep them from chattering, Sherry's resolve was firm. She saw Jon standing by the door and she told him, with no holds barred, what was on her mind.

"This one time, Agent Hatton," she said. "I will talk to Ms. Houze today, but that's it. I don't want any further details about the case or the women involved, or anything. You're going to need to find someone else."

His eyes narrowed the slightest bit, but then he nodded. "Call me Jon. And I understand. You're on vacation."

She was pretty sure he didn't understand anything. That he thought she was a spoiled brat who didn't care about anybody but herself. She could admit that bugged her, but she knew she had to take care of herself. Knew she had to find a way of getting past this coldness if she ever hoped to really work as a forensic artist again. Or at this point, to even be able to draw again ever.

Not having her art in her life was not an acceptable compromise.

A little warm, she pushed up her sleeves. At least talking to him had taken care of most of the chill. "That's right, I'm on vacation."

Let the jerk think what he wanted. She brushed past him on her way indoors. She was actually relieved to feel the air-conditioning.

"We need anything that Ms. Houze can give us," Jon told her as they walked down the hall. She noticed he already knew most of the nurses. They waved to him and immediately began whispering to each other. No doubt about the tall, dark-haired, gorgeous agent hallowing their hallways.

Let them have him.

"Anything," he repeated. "A full description of the perp's face would, of course, be optimal. But anything at all would be helpful."

Sherry nodded. "You probably shouldn't hope for too much." From me or her.

Jon grimaced. "I know you don't want to know anything about the case. But we have *nothing*, Sherry. This guy is really smart. So when I say anything Ms. Houze remembers, I mean anything. No matter how small."

"I'll do my best." As they arrived at Jasmine's door, Sherry explained how she worked. "I'm going to leave the door open, but I need you not to come inside. With a case like this, and especially after what happened yesterday with Spangler, it's important for you to stay out. Allow me to build a rapport with her."

"That's fine."

"Even if you feel like it's going too slowly or I'm asking questions that don't pertain to the case, you still don't get to butt in."

He looked a little affronted at that. Good. That was how she felt every time he muttered the word *vacation*.

"What I do takes time, so I hope you brought a *People* magazine or something," she continued.

He rolled his eyes. "How about if I just listen out here and take notes? I don't think a gossip magazine will be necessary."

"Fine. Just don't interrupt unless it's an emergency. No matter if you think I'm off target or missing something."

"I got it. No interruptions. Take as long as you need."

"She knows I'm coming, right? And that's okay with her?" After what had happened yesterday, Sherry wouldn't be surprised if the woman didn't want to see anyone from law enforcement again.

"Yes, we cleared it with her, although I think she is planning to have a family member in, just in case. I okayed it with the doctor, also, just before you got here."

"Fine." She looked at him again. "Just don't expect too much."

"Trust me." Jon's eyes were tight, frustrated. "Anything you can give us is better than where we are now."

"I'll do my best."

"That's all I can ask."

Sherry was afraid her best wasn't going to be anywhere near enough. She straightened her shoulders and walked into the room. This wasn't going to be pretty. But at least she wasn't cold.

THREE HOURS LATER Jon sat in the hallway outside Jasmine Houze's door. Sherry was wrapping it up, he could tell. She and Jasmine were talking about insignificant things: shoes, sales at different stores, favorite place to grab a margarita.

Really more than half of the time Sherry had spent with the woman had been used talking about seemingly insignificant things. Jon understood now why she had warned him not to interrupt. Obviously in the past she had been interrupted by people who thought she should be getting to the root of the issue—the actual drawing—more quickly.

While Jon could see why someone might jump to that conclusion, he wouldn't have interrupted today even if Sherry had never asked any questions about the attack. She very masterfully built a rapport with Jasmine. There had been nothing fake about it. Every question she had asked seemed sincere.

Jon didn't really know how well the woman could draw, but she could question a victim as well as, if not better than, many seasoned law-enforcement officers. Not just ones like Spangler who had no business being around victims. Sherry was excellent at what she did.

No wonder her supervisor held her in such high regard. She had patience, sincerity and an easygoing manner. Jon could tell just from hearing her talk. She knew when to press and when to back off. She'd let Ms. Houze tell her story in pieces, as she was ready, not ever forcing it, but gently bringing her back around to the questioning when they got too far off track.

What Sherry did with so much ease and naturalness couldn't be taught. She had instincts that were right on. As someone who also had pretty good instincts where most people were concerned, Jon was able to recognize it easily in Sherry.

Unfortunately, despite all of Sherry's interviewing abilities, Jon knew without even seeing, there was nothing she would've been able to draw. Jasmine Houze never saw her attacker's face and, despite Sherry cleverly questioning her from multiple different angles, never saw any distinguishing marks or any information that Sherry could've transferred onto paper in a way that would help them find the rapist.

Sherry had listened to Jasmine talk about the attack—details about it that had made him wince, and knew it had to have affected Sherry, also. Listening to such horror, and then subtly asking the poor victim to repeat it, was difficult.

For the first time Jon felt a little bad about how he'd mentally ripped into Sherry about the whole vacation thing. Her job as a forensic artist obviously was hard; that much was clear after listening to her for a couple of hours. No wonder she'd wanted a break from it for a little while as she was on vacation.

Although he knew she didn't want any more details about the case or to be involved in any way, after seeing how good she was today, Jon didn't think there was any way he was going to be able to let her walk away. Maybe if she would be willing to talk to the other victims. Maybe one of them would remember *something* that could lead to a crack in the case.

Hell, maybe Ms. Houze might still remember something. Talking to her again a few days from now would be customary in a case such as this.

Sherry should really be the one to do that, since she'd already built the rapport with her. It would be easier for everyone involved.

Except Sherry, of course.

Jon winced. Perhaps he could get her vacation extended or something. Or—and this didn't sit well with him, but he'd do it if he had to—maybe he could get her supervisor at the Bureau to put pressure on her to help with this case.

Either way Jon knew he needed to keep Sherry on this case with him. No matter what he had to do to make that happen.

He heard Sherry make her goodbyes to Jasmine and the two members of her family who had stayed in the room, wishing them all the best and promising that law enforcement was doing everything in its power to find the person responsible. Wishes and encouragement to stay strong. And to be sure to contact them if Jasmine thought of anything—even the smallest detail— she had forgotten before. To call anytime day or night. She even gave her personal number.

These were things Jon would say if he was in there, but he knew his presence there would just be intrusive.

Sherry backed out of the room, saying one last goodbye before pulling the door closed behind her, still facing it.

"Hey, you did amazing work in there," Jon said. "Honestly. I know she didn't remember anything, but—"

Jon cut himself off midsentence as Sherry turned to face him. Dear God, her lips were almost blue, her entire body completely tensed to keep from shaking.

"Sherry, what the hell?" Jon reached for her as she took a shaky step.

"I'm c-cold," she said.

"I see that. Is this one of your cold spells you were talking about?"

She nodded. He wrapped an arm around her and led her to a bench across the hall. He sat, holding her as close as possible, trying to transfer some of his body heat.

"Let me get one of the doctors to look at you."

"No, it'll pass. I've already seen a doctor. It's..." She trailed off. "It will pass."

"You're sure you're not sick?"

"Not physically." She tapped her head. "It's all in here."

"I don't really understand what you're saying." He was relieved to see her face was beginning to regain color and her shuddering was easing. They sat in silence for long moments as she gathered herself.

"This is why I'm on vacation. For the past few months every time I've done any work at all as a forensic artist, I've been overcome by these cold spells."

"What did your doctor say about them?" he asked, keeping her pinned to his side.

She looked away. "Well, I didn't actually tell him about them. I just had him do a complete physical so I was sure I didn't have a tumor or something. Since he deemed me in perfect health, yet I'm sometimes cold when it's ninety degrees out, I figured it must be psychological."

Jon didn't need to be a doctor to know what was going on here, and was sure her doctor could've figured it out if Sherry had given him all the information.

Sherry was suffering from some form of post-traumatic stress disorder. He had seen it in more than a few of his closest friends at Omega over the years, to varying degrees and with different symptoms. Some not totally dissimilar from what Sherry was experiencing.

Trauma affected the brain. Whether you experienced it firsthand or not, the brain could only take so much before it started taking measures to protect itself. Sherry's mind was trying to stop her from doing further damage to her psyche.

And the time she needed to heal was time Jon didn't have.

Chapter Seven

Two days later, sitting next to Caroline on the beach, Sherry was still considering what Jon had said to her in the hospital hallway. That she was suffering from some sort of post-traumatic stress.

Sherry had never even considered that; had thought that was only something that people who'd been in the military went through. After some research she realized she'd been wrong. Anybody who had experienced or witnessed a traumatic event could suffer from it.

Sherry was positive she didn't have PTSD. That was a serious, very real disorder that affected thousands of people, and she didn't want to take away from the very real trauma sufferers had gone through by comparing her situation to theirs.

But it gave her a starting place about what the heck was going on with her. A reassurance that she wasn't going crazy, but just needed to find some better coping mechanisms when it came to her job.

"So, did you say yes to Agent Handsome when he came calling the other day?" Caroline asked her from where she was perched in the sun.

Sherry had managed to work herself down to just shorts and a tank top over her bikini in the past two days. It wasn't perfect, but it was better. And at least now she felt she had somewhere to start when it came to this blasted coldness. Whenever she felt the least chill come on, she immediately turned her thoughts in a different direction. Anything that took her away from where her subconscious was going.

The thought of Jon Hatton generally skipped her past warm and straight to hot. Mostly because he was a jerk.

Although she had to admit that when she was so cold after the interview, he'd been very understanding and helpful. Had helped her fight the cold by keeping her close to his body.

Sherry sighed. "I didn't want to, but, yes, I did. He's pretty persuasive. Not to mention I could tell he thought I was the most selfish person on the planet when I resisted at first."

"He thought you were selfish because you wouldn't go out with him?"

Sherry put her sunglasses on top of her head and looked over at her friend. "First of all, how do you know about all this? Second of all, he didn't come by to ask me out, he came by to badger me into meeting with Jasmine Houze."

Caroline let loose a string of obscenities that was totally at odds with her young, sweet look.

Sherry laughed. "I take it you didn't know."

"He asked me where you were staying, but he said it was because he wanted to ask you out."

Sherry thought of how he had helped her at the hospital, kept her by his side until the iciness had passed. Then followed behind her as she'd driven home to make sure she made it all right. No, not a date, but perhaps he wasn't quite as bad as the string of obscenities suggested.

"Well, I think he needed my help more than he needed a date."

"I'm still going to let him have it next time I see him. I was so busy laughing at him when he suggested Zane and I might go on a date with you two that I wasn't really paying attention to anything else."

"What is it with you and Zane? The vibe between the two of you is crazy."

Caroline took another sip of her water, rolling her eyes. "Don't I know it? Zane and I are...complicated. It would just traumatize you further for me to talk about it. Traumatize me, too."

Sherry had told Caroline some of the stuff that had been going on with her: the cold spells and not being able to draw. Caroline was sympathetic and, as a paramedic, she was no stranger to trauma herself.

"How did it go with Jasmine Houze?"

Sherry shrugged. "As good as could be expected, considering she hadn't gotten any sort of look at her attacker."

"Damn it," Caroline muttered. "So you couldn't draw anything, after all."

"Yeah. Glad I didn't even have to try. As much as I'd like to help, I'm not sure I could've done anything useful."

Caroline grimaced. "Somebody's got to put a stop to this guy."

"Yeah, Jon said he's smart."

"So you actually talked to Jon? I thought you said he was a jerk."

"We talked a little bit about the case," Sherry said. "But to be honest, I didn't want any details. He just wanted to make sure I knew that no detail was too small when I was talking to Jasmine."

Caroline nodded. "You know, the crock about asking you out notwithstanding, I've found Jon to be a very stand-up guy. He talked to Michael, my partner, and me about the second victim. Asked our opinions about what had happened since we were first on the scene."

"Is that unusual?" Sherry asked.

"Well, neither Zane nor any of the other local detectives have ever asked my professional opinion, that's for sure. Too bad I didn't have anything interesting to share with Jon. But he still listened."

"Are we talking about the same Agent Hatton?"

Caroline laughed. "I'm just telling you, he isn't really a jerk."

"If you say so."

Caroline stood. "Okay, I'm off to shower before my shift."

"Okay, I'm going to hang here. Try to face the ol' sketch pad again." Sherry was feeling relaxed, warm. Ready to try. "You be safe out there tonight."

"Will do. Don't push it with the drawing. Let it come when it comes." They hugged and Sherry sent Caroline on her way.

That left Sherry alone with her sketch pad. She flipped to the first page and found the rough outline of Jon's face staring back at her.

Even without trying she had captured his dark good looks. Almost without conscious consent, her fingers took the pencil and began tracing in the details from his face onto the paper. As Caroline said, she didn't overthink it, just let it come.

Fifteen minutes later she had a full portrait of Jon looking back at her. Eyes faintly laced with disapproval, a slight scowl.

Yep, pretty much exactly as she remembered him. Jerk.

She had to admit, at least she wasn't cold. She

hadn't felt the iciness grip her bones even once while she was drawing him.

So evidently if she could just go around drawing Jon Hatton, she would be okay. Somehow she didn't think that was going to help her very much.

Her phone rang and Sherry looked at the number, one she didn't recognize. She debated on whether she should answer at all, but decided she would.

"Hello?"

"Ms. Mitchell?" It was a soft female voice, but Sherry didn't recognize it.

"Yes."

"This is Jasmine Houze. I'm sorry to bother you."

Sherry had given Jasmine her phone number at the hospital but honestly hadn't expected the other woman to use it. She figured Jasmine would've called Jon or one of the Corpus Christi detectives before calling her.

Sherry couldn't turn the woman away.

"No, you're not bothering me at all. Are you okay?"

"I'm as well as can be expected, I guess. They released me from the hospital this morning."

"That's good news, right?"

"I'm glad to be out, but I'm not ready to go to my h-house yet."

Sherry's heart broke at the woman's shaky

mention of her house. Sherry wasn't surprised she didn't want to go there. She wouldn't be surprised if Jasmine never lived in that house again.

"I totally understand. Do you have somewhere to stay?"

"Yeah, my mom and I are staying at my cousin's house, on the beach. It's not too far from my house. I feel okay there, as long as they're with me." Her words were still a little mushy, undoubtedly injury related.

"That's totally understandable," Sherry said. "You need to give yourself whatever time you need to heal. Don't let anybody rush you and don't allow yourself to get frustrated."

That advice sounded familiar.

"Yeah, the counselor at the hospital told me the same thing."

"That's because we're both brilliant."

That got a laugh, as Sherry had hoped it would.

"I don't mean to bother you, but you said to call if I thought of anything, no matter how small."

"Yes, I was absolutely serious about that. It really doesn't matter how insignificant it may seem."

"Well, this doesn't have anything to do with his face."

That was a little disappointing because, of course, any identifying facial feature would be a wonderful help. But facial features weren't the only things that could assist law enforcement.

"That's okay, Jasmine. His face isn't the only thing you might remember that can help the police. Maybe you should call them."

"I remember part of a tattoo on the inside of h-his arm." Sherry's heart broke as she heard Jasmine begin to cry. "And latex gloves. I don't know why I'm just remembering this now."

"That's okay. More than okay, Jasmine. Really good." A tattoo was something Sherry could draw. "Where is your cousin's house exactly? I can come over there, if you want me to. Draw whatever you remember of the tattoo."

"That would be so great." The relief was plain in the woman's voice. "I just want to get it out of my head."

Sherry very much understood being trapped in one's own head.

"Okay, give me your address. I'll just need to run home and get my car." Sherry had met Caroline on the beach halfway between their two houses so neither of them needed to drive.

She entered the address into her phone when Jasmine gave it to her and was surprised when she saw how close the house was to her present location.

"Actually, I'm only a couple of blocks from you right now. If you don't mind that I'm all sandy, I can be there much sooner if I just walk."

"Sooner is definitely better. I want to be sure I don't forget this."

Sherry was sure Jasmine wouldn't forget the tattoo. It would probably creep into her nightmares for the rest of her life. But there was no need to tell her that.

"Okay, I'll be there in just a few minutes."

They disconnected the call and Sherry began putting her items in her beach bag. Not too much stuff, thankfully: towel, sunscreen, her sketch pad and a few other items. She hadn't brought the umbrella, but she would need to carry her lightweight beach chair.

She categorically refused to think about the possibility that she wouldn't be able to draw what Jasmine described. She marched down the beach, focusing on the picture she'd drawn of Jon. Thinking about him seemed to keep her functional and definitely not cold. Whether that was because he made her mad or for other reasons, she wasn't going to delve into it too deeply.

It didn't take too long to walk to Jasmine's cousin's house, since it was a straight shot down the beach. The beach was mostly empty in the late-afternoon sun, early June being less crowded in the beach town since school had not yet let out. It was a nice walk, and for Sherry, pleasant in the heat.

As she finished the last few hundred yards to the house, Sherry could swear she felt someone watching her. She spun around, but saw no one except for a jogger far away from her headed the other way. She looked up at the houses that lined the street parallel to the beach, but didn't see anyone.

She took a deep breath as she felt cold starting to work its way through her system. She grabbed her long-sleeved shirt out of the bag and slipped it on, then walked more quickly toward the house.

This feeling was all in her imagination, Sherry knew. But she wished she had walked home and gotten her car, no matter that it would've taken longer.

Right now she needed to keep it together. Someone who had experienced something truly traumatic needed her help. The iciness and imaginary bogeyman watching her were nothing compared to the very real ugliness that made up Jasmine's reality.

Jasmine was sitting in a chair on the second-story deck of her cousin's house. No matter what it took, Sherry was going to focus on that brave woman up there and get through this.

Chapter Eight

Jon pulled up to the house where Jasmine was staying just as Sherry was coming down the outdoor back stairs from the second-story deck. Jasmine was behind her.

He'd been glad when Jasmine's mother called, had told him about Jasmine remembering the tattoo on the rapist's arm. Any identifying mark could help. Not only in finding and arresting the perpetrator, but also in the trial against him.

Maybe if she remembered this, there was hope that she might remember more; that her mind still held some secrets she wasn't aware of yet. Jon hoped so, because even after spending the past two days recombing the crime scene and recanvassing the neighborhood, they still didn't have any leads.

He hadn't been able to get Sherry Mitchell out of his mind. Yes, he wanted her professional opinion and artistic abilities on the case. But more than that, he just wanted to see her again.

To see if she was doing any better after that debilitating cold spell she'd suffered at the hospital.

Yet he had known that if he contacted her, his concern would've come across as professional rather than personal. That he was making sure she was okay so she could help him with this case, not because he actually cared what happened to her.

He did have a professional concern for her, definitely. If there was some way he could help her so that she could in turn use her artist and interviewing skills to help them capture this guy, Jon was more than willing to do that.

But he'd also like to help her because he couldn't stop thinking about her. About her gorgeous long legs, gorgeous blond hair, gorgeous blue eyes.

And the fragility that seemed to surround her. As if she might shatter at any moment.

That was the real reason Jon hadn't stopped back by to see Sherry even though he'd wanted to and desperately wanted her for the case.

She wasn't ready.

If Jon kept pushing—and he knew it was in his nature to do so—then all he'd be doing was creating another victim as a result of this violence. Until Sherry's mind was ready for her to get back to work on the case, Jon didn't want to force it if there were any other options. He already had his boss at Omega looking for other forensic artists. Steve would come up with someone.

Jon was surprised Sherry was here, since Jasmine's mom hadn't mentioned it, and knowing how Sherry felt about getting involved. After seeing the toll working with victims took on her, Jon couldn't have blamed her for just hunkering down under her beach umbrella and never facing anything again.

He'd been wrong about her. She wasn't spoiled; she was protecting herself.

So he already admired the fact that she was here at all. He walked over to where she and Jasmine were talking at the bottom of the outdoor staircase.

"Ladies." He said it while he was still far enough away not to startle Jasmine. He could see how Sherry immediately tensed at his voice.

"Hi, Agent Hatton," Jasmine said. Her face was still bruised, but not nearly as swollen as it had been two days ago.

"How are you feeling?" he asked her.

The young woman shrugged. "Afraid to go out by myself. Afraid of the dark. Afraid to set foot in my own home. So, not great."

Sherry took her hand. "It's okay to be afraid of all those things. You might always be, and that's okay, too."

"Yeah, well, none of that is as bad as when the doorbell rings. Poor package delivery guy must have thought everybody in the house was crazy. Doorbell rang and I totally freaked out. Then my mom and cousin started crying. All he wanted to do was deliver some shoes my cousin ordered a few days ago."

Jon met Sherry's eye. It was a hard story for either of them to hear. They both knew Jasmine's attacker had rung her doorbell and then forced his way in when she'd cracked open the door.

Jon wanted to comfort Jasmine but knew he couldn't. There was only so much he could do. Sherry, on the other hand, was more easily able to, and reached out to touch the other woman.

"You know what?" Sherry said to Jasmine, rubbing the woman's arm lightly. "Have your cousin disconnect the doorbell. Disconnect it at your house when you go back there. *If* you decide to go back there. Or, if you decide to move into another place, disconnect the doorbell there. Disconnect the damn doorbell at every place you live for the rest of your life. That's *okay*."

"It just seems so cowardly." Jasmine's voice was small.

"No." Both he and Sherry said it at the same time.

"Not cowardly at all," Jon continued.

"You don't ever have to apologize for how you choose to survive," Sherry said. "You need to heal on your timetable, not anyone else's. Taking tiny, little baby steps is still forward progress."

"You're up, outside, talking. That's more than many would be in your situation," Jon said.

"Thanks, you guys. I think I'm going to go in and rest. Describing that tattoo took more out of me than I thought." Jasmine turned to Sherry. "Can you show it to Agent Hatton?"

"Sure, no problem."

Jasmine looked at Jon. "That's okay, right? I just don't want to look at it again right now."

"Absolutely fine. Sherry will go over all the details with me. You don't worry about it."

"Yes, just rest, Jasmine," Sherry said. "If you think of anything else, I'm more than happy to come back."

Jasmine nodded before making her way up the outdoor stairs to where her mother and cousin were waiting. Jon was glad to see she had a good support network. That made a huge difference in the healing process.

He turned back to Sherry. "I realize it was probably difficult for you to come here and that you don't want to be involved in this case. But I appreciate it anyway."

Sherry stiffened. "I didn't do it for you. I did it for that brave woman up there."

"Either way, I still appreciate it. I realize that it still probably took a toll on you, regardless of who you did it for, so thank you."

Sherry nodded. "It wasn't as bad as I thought it might be."

But she still had her long-sleeved shirt on, even in the early-evening heat, so it had been at least somewhat bad.

"Did Jasmine remember anything particularly useful?" he asked her.

"Well, his skin was dark. That's one thing she remembers."

"Like African-American?"

"No, but not fair-skinned. Maybe Mexican or Latin American descent." Sherry brought out the sketch pad she had tucked under one arm. "Basically she remembered his hands. He had on some sort of latex or rubber gloves."

"That's not surprising at all, considering the lack of evidence that has been left at the scenes. If you told me he had wrapped his entire body in some sort of protective gear, I wouldn't be surprised."

Sherry opened her sketch pad to the page she was looking for. There she'd drawn an arm stretched at an odd angle. The latex gloves covered his fingers and hand up to his wrist, but then farther up, peaking through the sleeve hole of a white office shirt, was a tattoo of a skull with two bull's-eyes in the eye sockets. Not big enough to be something overtly noticeable in everyday life, but certainly something identifiable.

"Interesting ink," Jon murmured. "First thing I'll do is have Corpus Christi PD run it against any known gang marks."

Sherry nodded. "I've become familiar with some gang tattoos in my two years working cases in the Southeast and don't recognize this, but my knowledge is in no way exhaustive."

"Does she remember anything else about that shirt?"

"No, just that it was a white cuff, like any normal shirt a man would wear to an office or something, she said. She only remembers it was white because of the thought that his skin was so dark."

Jon looked at the picture again. "His arm seems to be at a weird angle."

"Yeah, that's how Jasmine described it. I walked her through it a couple of times to be sure. I think it is because of how she was thrown on the ground. But it works to our advantage because if his arm had been at a more natural angle, she wouldn't have seen the tattoo."

"That's good. Or as good as something can be in a situation like this." He noticed Sherry was worrying her lip with her teeth, studying the picture. After a few seconds he forced his attention away from her lips. Barely. "Is there something wrong?"

She shrugged. "It's just not my best work. I can see where…"

He waited for her to continue, but she didn't.

"Where you what?"

"Just where I was starting to have my cold spells again. Lines are shaky, not as crisp."

"It looks fine to me."

"In this situation, I think it is okay, since a hand is a hand. If I had been drawing someone's facial features, needing as much detail as possible? Those little errors could've made the difference between the drawing bearing a true resemblance to the perpetrator and just being a generic face that wouldn't do law enforcement any good." She was back to gnawing on her lip.

"Was the cold bad?" Before he could stop himself, he reached up and stroked her lip with his thumb so she wouldn't cause it any harm with her teeth.

Their eyes met for just a moment—a heat-filled moment—before Sherry looked away and he dropped his hand. At least she stopped hurting that soft lip. If she needed anyone to nibble on it, he'd be glad to do that for her.

Although suggesting it would probably not go over well.

She had stopped talking altogether. "I'm sorry, please continue. I just didn't want you to injure that lip."

"Oh." To his surprise, a delicate flush covered her cheek. She continued. "The cold was only bad when I could feel Jasmine's terror."

"That's understandable."

"I tried to focus on her, which was both good and bad. It made it that much harder to hear her story and know she was so frightened. On the other hand, I tried to focus on the fact that I was fine. I am not the one who'd had this horrible event happen to me. The least I could do was man up and listen without freaking out."

Jon couldn't help smiling at *man up*. "You made it through."

"Only because she had very little to remember and it was ninety degrees outside. I don't know what I would've done otherwise."

"I'm sure you would've handled that, too. Woman up'ed. That's one step beyond manning up."

A little of her tension eased. She actually smiled at him.

The beauty of it struck him unexpectedly. Made him want to do things he wouldn't normally consider with a woman he'd only known a few days. Jon liked to think pretty carefully before he leaped into any sort of relationship.

But her smile made him feel that thinking was overrated.

He realized he was seeing her as she was meant to be: relaxed, smiling, easy. Probably how she had been before these panic attacks had started taking over.

She began closing up her sketch pad but not before Jon caught a glimpse of the drawing she'd made of him. He stopped her.

Wow. She'd done a lot of work on this since he'd

seen it a couple of days ago on the beach. He had thought it was good then, but this was amazing.

"This is incredible." He didn't know a drawing could look so realistic. She had shaded it in and added depth and perspective. It was almost like looking at a black-and-white photo of himself.

She had truly captured his likeness.

She tried to take the pad from him, but he stepped to the side, still looking at the drawing. "Have you been working on this for the past two days?"

"No, Agent Hatton. Believe it or not, I do have other things in my life. I did it in about thirty minutes this afternoon."

Oh, great, now they were back to Agent Hatton. But Jon couldn't get past the drawing.

"You did this in less than an hour? From memory?"

"Just give me the damn pad."

She was embarrassed. It was kind of endearing how color stained her cheeks once again. Jon liked it so much better than her face being pinched and pale. She also looked as though she might slug him, so he handed her the sketch pad.

"You're really talented."

"Thanks. Right now it's hit or miss, I'm afraid. I was able to draw this by not focusing on any cases or anything upsetting. That's much harder when you're listening to someone talk about horrific things that happened to them."

"It's at least a start, right? You actually drew something."

Sherry shrugged. "I guess so."

"I don't want to push you to do more than you're ready to do, but if you start feeling able, I'd love your help with this case. Maybe not talking to the other victims, just looking over what Frank Spangler got from them, which wasn't much. See if there's anything he missed. If you think you're up to it."

Chapter Nine

Was she up to it?

Sherry just didn't know. She had made it through the past hour with Jasmine, but just barely. She had drawn that picture of Jon today, but had deliberately kept her mind neutral as she did so.

One thing she knew for sure, she didn't seem to feel cold around Jon Hatton, whether it was anger or attraction.

What wasn't to be attracted to? His dark looks, soft hazel eyes and chiseled chin were etched in her subconscious—she knew that from how quickly she had drawn him. Not to mention height. There weren't many men who made her feel tiny and feminine.

Jon Hatton did. Everything about him made her just want to ease a little closer.

"Just ease into it, you know? As you're ready. Might be good for you, too."

"What?" Sherry had to stop herself from jumping backward. Had she said something out loud about how attractive she found him?

Jon was looking at her funny. "Helping with the cases? Just a little bit at a time?"

Easing into *cases*. Yes. Right.

"Um, yeah, maybe. But right now I've got to get going." Before she did something completely stupid such as tell him how attractive he was and how she very definitely didn't feel cold when she was around him.

"Okay, where's your car?" He reached down to take her beach bag. "I'll put this in it for you."

"I don't have a car. I walked here."

"You *what*?" Jon's tone noticeably deepened.

"I walked from Caroline's house. It's about halfway between where I'm staying and here."

"And you're just going to *walk* home?" If possible his voice deepened even more. And a vein was beginning to bulge a little in his forehead.

"It's only a little over a mile if you walk straight down the beach."

"Are you crazy?"

Now veins were bulging in his forehead and throat. "There's a rapist wandering around Corpus Christi and you think it is okay to just walk home, completely alone?"

Sherry remembered the feeling she'd gotten earlier walking on the beach. As if someone were watching her. Maybe walking alone hadn't been the best plan. "From what I've read, the attacks occurred at houses, not out on a beach in plain sight."

"There's still no way in hell I'm going to let you do something as idiotic as walk home as it's getting dark." His voice wasn't a shout, but it was definitely louder than normal conversation.

The craziness of it all was that Sherry didn't actually disagree with him. She'd be damned if she'd cower just because he was being a jerk.

Again.

"You know if you had just said, 'Why don't I give you a ride home? Now might not be the safest time to be walking alone,' I would've gladly accepted your offer. But now I think I'd rather take my chances alone than be stuck with you."

Jon ran a hand over his face. She could see him attempting to reboot and get the situation and himself under control.

"Attempting to activate normal people mode, rather than jerk mode?" she asked him, aware that she probably shouldn't taunt him. He just made her so mad.

He grimaced but actually chuckled. "Believe it or not, I am actually known for my way with people. I'm a pretty friendly and likable guy."

"That's good to know. So I guess I won't have to suggest personality dialysis."

This time he laughed out loud. "You're a smart ass."

"So I've been told. But not in a long while."

It felt good to be irritated and attracted and warm. For too long she'd felt nothing but cold and fear.

"Why don't I give you a ride home?" Jon repeated her earlier words back to her. "Now might not be the safest time to be walking alone." He gave her a sparkling smile, the dimple in his chin irresistible in the fading light.

"Since I don't want to traumatize the Houze family any more than they've already been by yelling more out here, I accept."

As if there was any way she could resist that dimple.

He took her bag and put it in the backseat, then held the passenger door open for her.

The streets back to her house took a little while longer since there were no direct routes that ran parallel to the beach.

"Personality dialysis." He muttered it under his breath, shaking his head.

Yeah, that hadn't been nice. "Sorry," she said. "Growing up I had a tendency to blurt out whatever I was thinking."

"Trust me. I'll take my chances with your acerbic wit over seeing you suffer through those cold spells any day."

He reached over to grab her hand that was sitting between them in a friendly squeeze. They both felt the heat immediately when they touched.

Her eyes met his briefly before he turned back to the road and she put her hands in her lap.

Wow. That had never happened before. Sherry could almost still feel heat running through her fingers where they'd touched.

"Weird," she murmured.

He glanced over at her, but she couldn't read the expression in his eyes. "Yeah, weird."

There was silence for a few moments until she realized he wasn't going in the right direction for her house.

"Do you mind if we go into town and grab a sandwich? I haven't had dinner and have been all but dreaming about this barbecue brisket sandwich I had to part ways with a couple of days ago when called in for the case."

Sherry smiled. She could understand the appeal. "As long as they don't mind me coming in my beach wear."

Jon winked at her. "I'm pretty sure that won't be a problem at this place. They line the tables with newspaper." He made a turn leading them away from the beach. "Did you need anything from Caroline's house?"

"No, I have everything with me. She's working a night shift, so she's not home."

"Okay."

"Plus, she's pretty mad at you." As soon as she said the words, Sherry immediately saw the trap she'd laid for herself and wished she could take them back.

"What? Why?"

Sherry shrugged. "I don't know. Something you said or something."

"When? I would hate to think I've offended her. She's the one who has kept me in the loop when most of Corpus Christi PD has been trying to keep me out of it."

"It's nothing. She's not really mad. Forget I mentioned it."

"No, tell me." His tone brooked no refusal.

"It's nothing, seriously. You just told Caroline you were going to ask me out the other day."

He immediately knew what she was talking about. "Yeah, I told her that to get the address of where you were staying."

Hearing him admit that he'd never had any intention of actually asking her out hurt a little more than it should for someone she'd only known a few days.

She slid a little farther away from him in her seat. "Yeah, well, Caroline figured that out, so you better watch your back."

"Listen, it's not that I didn't want to ask you out. Just at the time, I needed you more for the case."

"And you knew how to work the situation to get what you wanted. How to work her and how to work me. You're pretty good at your job."

Jon glanced over at her, lips pinched together, driving in silence for another ten minutes until they pulled up at the diner. He still didn't say anything as he chose a parking space that was far away from the entrance in a darkened corner of the lot.

He parked and snatched the keys out of the transmission. In the same breath, he turned to her, leaning so far forward that Sherry had to lean back a little so they wouldn't be pressed together.

"You know what I'm good at?" he said. "I'm good at seeing things other people miss. I'm good at juggling multiple problems at the same time. I'm good at helping keep the press at bay and helping keep people from panicking in a situation like this one where it would be justifiable to do so."

He was upset. He didn't raise his voice, his veins weren't standing out in his forehead like when she mentioned walking home, but he seemed to be toeing a thin line with his control.

"You know what I'm not good at?" he continued. "Trying to balance the fact that I need your skills on this case with the overwhelming urge to keep you as far away from it as possible so that you can heal. I'm not good at constantly weighing what's good for the case versus what's good for you, instead of just—what did you call it the other day?—*handling* you to get what I want."

Sherry knew she should do something: get out, crack a joke, tell him to find another forensic artist. But all she could do was stare at him. As if she were hypnotized by his hazel eyes.

"Most of all I'm not good at being able to get you out of my mind. Damned if you haven't been stuck there since the first second I saw you."

His lips were on hers before she could form another thought.

If she thought there was heat when their hands had touched, this was downright explosive.

His mouth was wet, hot, open against hers and she couldn't get enough. Couldn't get close enough.

Forget cold. Within seconds she was *burning*. She forgot everything but the strength and heat of the kiss. It was consuming her.

Her fingers tangled in his hair, pulling him closer. She could feel his at her waist, hips, pulling her to him.

The loud ringing of a phone moments later was what forced them to ease back from each other. Their eyes locked, both downright dazed.

Jon finally reached down into the cup holder and picked up the phone. He looked at it then cursed under his breath. "It's Zane Wales from Corpus Christi PD. I've got to take this."

Sherry nodded.

"Hatton."

He listened to whatever Zane said and muttered another curse. He opened the car door and got out.

Sherry opened her door. It was positively steaming inside the car and for once she needed to cool herself down.

"Where?" Jon was saying. Then listened some more.

"I'll be right there. And for God's sake, make sure Spangler isn't around." He disconnected the call and looked straight at Sherry. "I'm sorry. You can't make an honest man out of me tonight. I've got to go."

"Trouble?" She hoped not.

He nodded, lips pursed. "Another woman has been attacked."

Sherry closed her eyes. When would this end?

"I'll take you home, then head out to the hospital. After what happened last time, I feel like I need to make sure no one upsets the victim in any way."

"I'll just come with you to the hospital. If you have to take me all the way home, it will be over thirty minutes before you get there. Maybe more."

"Are you sure?"

No, she wasn't sure at all. But she knew he needed to get there as soon as he could. "I don't think I'm ready to talk to this new victim, but I do want to help you get there as fast as possible."

He trailed a finger down her cheek. "Thank you. I know just being there isn't easy for you."

"I'll be all right. There's someone who has gone through much worse than me. Let's get you there so you can help her."

Chapter Ten

They pulled up at the hospital and rushed inside. Zane was waiting for them at the door, cowboy hat still firmly on his head, fairly brimming with excitement.

"We've got DNA," he told them without any greeting. "One of the nurses told me this latest victim was able to get a scratch in and there were definitely skin cells under her fingernails."

Jon was excited but surprised. "What sort of injuries does she have? Craniofacial trauma like the others?"

Zane was giddy. "No, just a couple of bruises, from what I understand. Guy was wearing a ski mask or something, so I don't think she got to see his face. Unfortunately."

"A mask? None of the other victims have mentioned a mask," Jon noted as they walked down the hall, Sherry on one side of him, Zane on the other.

"None of the other victims got a look at the perp. This is our lucky break, Hatton."

Jon reserved judgment. There was nothing he'd like more than a lucky break in this case. But he had a sinking feeling that this wasn't it.

Jon found himself back down the same hospital trauma hallway where he'd met Sherry a few days before. She was quiet, but at least this time she wasn't pale and shivering.

"Doing okay?" he murmured to her as they walked.

She nodded, and he reached down and grabbed her hand, giving it a supportive squeeze. She squeezed back before they both let go.

"We're waiting for Dr. Rosemont to come out and give us a report. Captain heard about the DNA and that the patient was conscious and is on his way over."

No doubt the man wanted to be here if there was going to be a big break in the case and press involved. Jon shook his head. He'd be glad to let Captain Harris get as much attention as he could handle as long as it meant they were stopping whoever was responsible.

They could hear yelling from inside the patient's room before they even got to the door. A woman's voice, shrieking.

"Someone thought they could do this to me? Thought they could just throw me down on the ground and attack me?"

Someone murmured something to her, but Jon couldn't hear what they said.

"Yes, I know he had every intention of raping me. But I didn't let him. I just kept hitting and punching."

Jon looked over at Zane with one eyebrow raised. "Sounds like she's not injured too much; not like the other victims."

Zane smiled. "Yeah. Seems like the SOB messed with the wrong woman this time."

"Did he break into her house or building like the others?" Jon asked.

"No." Zane shook his head. "I haven't confirmed this yet with the victim, but I think he was waiting for her at her work. Dragged her out of her car in the back of the parking lot."

Another discrepancy. Jon had to admit, their guy hadn't tended to follow an MO, so maybe it was their serial rapist who'd also committed this crime.

Sherry had taken a step back at the sound of the yelling. Jon stopped to talk to her.

"I'm going get a uniformed officer to take you home."

"No, I'm okay."

"Hey, it makes you uncomfortable to be here, and that's okay." He lowered his voice so Zane couldn't hear him. "I've got to be honest, I'm not even sure we're dealing with the same perpetrator here."

"Really?"

"I won't know until I talk to the victim and check out the scene, but…"

"There are some indications."

"Exactly. And if the attacker was wearing a ski mask, there won't be much for you to draw."

Sherry nodded. "Okay, then if you really don't mind, I guess I'd rather go home. I can call a cab."

"No, there will be plenty of officers that can give you a ride." He took her by the arm and led her toward the nurses' station. "If I need you, I'll call."

"Okay." Her voice was quiet, reserved.

"Actually, I'll be calling you tomorrow regardless. You have to make an honest man out of me before I talk to Caroline again. Have dinner with me tomorrow night, so it's true that I asked you out."

He thought about their kiss and how much more he wanted than just dinner, but that was a good place to start. If she would even agree to a real date.

"No manipulating or yelling, I promise," he said.

She smiled. "And I won't walk through the city alone."

Jon reached his hand out to shake hers. "Deal."

He walked her the rest of the way over to the

nurses' station. Sara Beth Carreker, the head nurse from the other day, was working.

"I have to admit, I'm sorry to see you back here again this week, Agent Hatton."

"I'm sorry to see me back here, too, Sara Beth, under these circumstances. This is my friend Sherry. Is it okay if she stays here until one of the uniformed officers gives her a ride home?"

"Sure, I'll be going in with the new victim, but some of the other nurses will be here. And Dr. Trumpold." She pointed at a handsome doctor standing at the counter, going through charts.

Dr. Trumpold shrugged. "I don't think—none of us think—it's very prudent for a male doctor to be in with a sexual assault victim, especially in the first few days."

"I guess that makes your job harder," Sherry said to him.

"It's okay. I understand. Whatever is best for the patients." The doctor smiled at Sherry.

Suddenly leaving Sherry here didn't seem like such a great idea to Jon, but he swallowed that down.

"I'm going to get back down the hall," Jon said and, unable to stop himself, put his arm around her in a sideways hug.

But call it what it really was: a claiming. Jon ignored the relief he felt when she leaned into him and smiled. "If someone hasn't come to take you home in ten minutes, come find me," he said.

Sherry nodded. "It's okay if you need to call me if the victim remembers seeing anything. I can't promise results, but I can at least try," she said.

"Are you a police officer?" Dr. Trumpold asked. "I saw you here the other day, but thought you were friends with the victim."

"No, I'm a forensic artist. Well, actually, I'm just on vacation. Evidently, I don't know what I am doing."

"You're healing, that's what you're doing." Jon reached down quickly and kissed her on the cheek. "The rest…we'll just see. See you tomorrow."

Just that brief touch of his lips—a friendly gesture by most counts—caused heat to flow through both of them. Sherry's eyes met his before darting nervously to Dr. Trumpold, who had politely turned away and started going through files.

"Tomorrow," Jon whispered again, and she nodded.

He turned and walked down the hall. He asked the first Corpus Christi officer he saw to find someone to get Sherry home. He was glad she wasn't staying. She wasn't comfortable. And he wasn't comfortable with her spending too much time with the handsome trauma doctor. Hopefully he had other cases he'd be attending to soon.

Captain Harris and Zane were standing outside the victim's room talking to Dr. Rosemont when Jon joined them.

"Ms. Grimaldi was very fortunate," the doctor was saying. "Especially compared to some of the other rape victims. Although undoubtedly the attacker meant her harm, he was not successful in his rape attempt. Nor did she suffer the same craniofacial trauma as the other victims."

"She was able to scratch the attacker?" Captain Harris asked.

The doctor nodded. "Yes, on the upper arm. The nurse will be out momentarily with the evidence that was collected."

"We'll rush this through and hopefully it will be a hit," the captain said. "Then we'll be able to put this nightmare behind us."

"Captain," Jon interrupted, "I don't think we should be too quick to make any assumptions. Even if you do get a DNA hit, it might not be the same guy as the others."

The captain stood there shaking his head at Jon for long seconds. "You know what we really don't need now, Hatton? Some sort of better-than-you outsider who's playing devil's advocate and doesn't really understand our community at all. People here are in a panic and they need to know immediately if we've caught this monster."

"I agree about people being in a panic." Jon tried to keep his voice level, but damned if he wasn't tired of this *outsider* trash. "I just think it would be prudent to be positive before we make any public announcements about the rapist being arrested."

The captain leaned forward, his lips pressed together in a thin line. "If I can give the people of Corpus Christi a good night's rest for the first time in weeks, I'm not going to deny them that just because you're a bureaucrat who wants to wrap everything in red tape, making it impossible for real police work to be done."

Jon counted to ten silently in his head in an effort not to tell the chief where he could go. Jon's specialty—hell, Omega Sector's specialty—was cutting through red tape, not adding it. Just because Jon refused to jump in to the hooray-we-caught-the-bad-guy party without any evidence did not make him a bureaucrat.

Jon turned toward the doctor. "Do you feel that Ms. Grimaldi is up for any questioning tonight?"

"She's scared, of course, but feels very lucky that she was able to fight off her attacker. I'll ask if she's willing to talk to you." The doctor went back into the room as a nurse came out with a bag of evidence.

Zane took it from her. "I'll go have this run immediately, Captain."

"You tell them to put every rush possible on it, Wales. And leave someone there so that as soon as the results are in we are notified." The captain looked over at Jon, pointedly. "Tonight, if possible."

Zane left, sprinting down the hall. Despite his words earlier, Jon prayed they would get a hit off the DNA and that it really was the serial rapist who had made a mistake with this victim.

Dr. Rosemont returned. "Ms. Grimaldi will see you and seems up for it. In light of what happened last time, I'm going to stay in the room."

Jon wasn't offended. After what had happened last time, the doctor was right to protect her patient. "Thanks."

The moment Jon walked into the room he became convinced this wasn't the attack of the same man. The woman had only one bruise on the side of her face and it was on the lower part of her chin.

The serial rapist had consistently aimed for the eyes first. The blows to the face had been purposeful in nature: to cause his victims not to be able to see or to identify him.

"Ms. Grimaldi, I'm so sorry for what happened to you tonight. If it's okay, we'd like to ask you a few questions?" Jon said.

She nodded and grabbed the hand of the woman—sister? friend?—sitting next to her. "Okay."

Dana Grimaldi was in her early thirties, Jon would estimate. She had blond hair, obviously not her natural color with the dark brown showing at the roots, and was of medium height and build. The serial rapist hadn't stuck to any one MO when choosing the demographics of his victims, so Jon had to admit that she could've fit the bill there.

"I'm Captain Harris from the Corpus Christi PD." The other man spoke up. "I don't normally work cases like this, but I'm here to personally help get this solved for you as soon as possible. Can you walk through what happened?"

"I was working a shift out at the harbor yard. I'm an administrative assistant for one of the companies at the port, so my hours aren't the same hours as the people who work the line, but they're pretty similar. A lot of times I have to walk in and out of the parking lot by myself. In the afternoon, when I get there, it's not a problem, but at night..."

The woman began crying. The other woman scooted closer and wrapped an arm around her. "You've told them about it. I know you have," the woman murmured.

Ms. Grimaldi looked up at Jon and Captain Harris. "I *have* told my supervisors how unsafe I feel walking out there alone. Where I have to park is usually way in the back. It's isolated from the rest of the parking lot by a line of Dumpsters."

"What did your company say when you told them?" the captain asked her.

It was a good question. Maybe there would be cameras that the company had available. It wouldn't help poor Ms. Grimaldi in what had happened to her, but it would possibly help capture who had done this.

"They said that any of the security guards would gladly walk me out to my car if I wanted them to. That warehouse is huge and finding a security guard sometimes isn't that easy. So I just went by myself." She started crying again, painful sobs. "I was so stupid."

"Hey," Jon said, taking a slow step toward her so as not to spook her unnecessarily. "Just because you walked there by yourself doesn't make this your fault. You could've walked across that parking lot in nothing but skimpy lingerie and that still wouldn't make it okay for someone to attack you. *His* fault. *He's* the one to blame. Not you."

She nodded, tears subsiding a little.

"Tell us what happened next."

"I got into my car. I left the door open once I sat down because it was so hot in the car from sitting in the parking lot all afternoon. I was turning to get my phone out of my purse when the guy reached in and grabbed me." She clung to the other woman.

"He pulled me up out of the car by my shirt, ripping it, and then threw me against the side of the car. He was wearing a mask, so I couldn't see his face."

Jon looked over at Captain Harris. The man had to realize how different this victim's story was than the stories they had heard over the past few weeks. No immediate blows to the face? A mask? At a car instead of inside a building?

"All I could think was about that rapist who was on the loose. We'd all been told not to open our doors to strangers, but I hadn't heard about anything in parking lots. I knew what he was going to do—going to try to do—so I just started fighting like a crazy person."

"You were able to scratch your attacker?" the captain asked.

She nodded. "Yes, although I didn't really notice it at the time. I think it was his arm because that was the only place where I saw skin. I was just trying to scream my head off and get away if I could.

"He hit me when I screamed, right on the jaw, but I just kept screaming and swinging and kicking the best I could. And he just ran away. Some other people heard me and they came running up not long afterward. Called the police and ambulance, and they brought me here."

Her breaths were coming much heavier, but she made it through the story.

"It sounds like you were very brave and did everything right," Jon assured her.

"I was so scared. Now I'm angry, but then I was just scared."

"I can imagine," Captain Harris said. "We're going to use the DNA from when you scratched him and hopefully be able to make an arrest soon. Even tonight."

Jon shook his head. Harris still wanted to run with this being the serial rapist. After hearing Dana's story, Jon was convinced more than ever that—very fortunately for Dana—the man who attacked her wasn't the rapist they'd been searching for.

This was some sort of copycat.

Chapter Eleven

"Ms. Grimaldi, is there anyone that you know of that might want to hurt you in some way? Any ex-boyfriends or husbands or friends that are mad at you? Fights you have had with anyone?"

Harris glared at Jon at the question, but he didn't care. Even though it probably wasn't the serial rapist, Ms. Grimaldi had still been attacked and this was still a case that needed to be solved.

"I broke up with my boyfriend a couple of weeks ago. He was pretty upset. But I know he didn't do this. He's not that type of person."

Jon knew that heartbreak and rage could turn people into someone different. Unrecognizable. He got the man's name and address from the victim. Tony Shefferly.

"Hopefully just to eliminate him as a suspect," Jon told her. Any scratches on his arms would help confirm or eliminate him from their suspect pool.

Since she hadn't seen much because of his

mask and the attack, thank God, had not progressed to an actual rape, there weren't many other questions that either Jon or Captain Harris had to ask. Jon turned to leave, but Harris went back, offering his hand out to Dana to shake.

"Your bravery is going to be key in helping us catch this monster who has terrorized our city, Ms. Grimaldi. Thank you for that. We'll be back in touch."

Ms. Grimaldi looked elated at Harris's words. Jon bit his tongue to keep from saying anything. Bringing up the holes in the captain's theory in front of the victim was not a good idea.

As he was going out the door, there was one last thing Jon knew he needed to ask her, based on what Sherry had learned from Jasmine Houze earlier.

"You didn't see any tattoos on the man's arms, did you? About halfway up between his wrist and elbow?"

Dana shook her head. "No, I don't remember seeing anything like that."

"What about gloves? Was the man who attacked you wearing any sort of gloves? Latex or otherwise?"

Dana shuddered. "No, he definitely wasn't wearing gloves. I remember feeling his hands on my arms when he pushed me down on the ground. Definitely no gloves."

"Okay, thanks again for your help. No matter what happens in this investigation, Captain Harris is right, you were certainly very brave."

Jon pulled the door closed behind him when he exited the room to find Captain Harris glaring at him.

"What the hell was that about, Hatton? 'No matter what happens in this investigation.' Are you trying to make me look like a fool?"

No, the older man was taking all the steps to do that himself without any help from Jon. "Captain, I'm trying to be objective here. I don't think this is the same guy."

"What were those questions about the tattoo and gloves?"

"I found out earlier today that Jasmine Houze remembered something. A tattoo on the inside of her attacker's arm. Also, that he was wearing latex gloves."

"You met with a victim without anybody from the department with you?" His nostrils flared.

"No, actually, Ms. Houze called Sherry Mitchell, the forensic artist Omega found to replace Frank Spangler. Ms. Mitchell met with the victim and provided me with the sketch of the tattoo. I was bringing it in to check against possible gang tattoos when I got the call about Ms. Grimaldi's attack."

That was almost true except for the part where he and Sherry almost set his car on fire from the heat between them. That definitely didn't need to be mentioned to Captain Harris.

"Well, Grimaldi could neither confirm nor deny the tattoo, so that doesn't help us one way or another," Captain Harris responded.

Jon shook his head. "Captain, I respect that you love your city and want to keep it safe. I know you want this guy behind bars so you can assure the people looking to you that the Corpus Christi PD has done its job and has gotten a monster off the street."

"Yeah, so?"

"Part of the reason I was sent here was to help with crisis management. As someone with experience in that area, I'm asking you not to make any formal statements to the press, even if we are able to arrest someone from the DNA findings, until we can definitively link Ms. Grimaldi's case to those of other women."

"Damn it, Hatton…"

"We don't have to link it to all the other cases, just one, and I'll be satisfied." Jon held a hand out in a gesture of peace. "There are too many discrepancies. She was attacked in a parking lot instead of a building. She wasn't immediately struck in the face like the others. The guy wore a ski mask and no gloves."

"None of those things mean it wasn't our perp."

"I agree. But taking all of the facts together

gives enough reasonable doubt that it may not be. To report to the press that the suspect is in custody, only to find out—from another woman being raped—that we have the wrong person? As your crisis-management representative, I wanted to tell you that would be a nightmare in terms of community relations."

"Fine," Harris said. "No one will make any official statements about anything until we have evidence linking him to the other cases."

"Thank you, Captain."

"If I'm right, and we are able to link all the rapes to this one guy and the city of Corpus Christi spent more days in worry when it could've been sleeping soundly? I'll expect you to make an announcement to the press that it was the feds' call to do that."

"Fine." Jon didn't have any real concern that would be necessary, but if it kept the captain from making a pretty big mistake, he was willing to risk it.

Captain Harris wasn't mollified. "And it's not like the other part of your job you were sent for— behavioral analysis of this bastard—has been of any use."

Jon didn't have much response to that. "You're right. He's been one step ahead of all of us the whole time. He's made no mistakes. That is part of the reason why this last case, with all its many mistakes, has me thinking it's not the same guy."

Zane Wales came running down the hall. "We've got a hit through the DNA. Perp has a record. Uniforms are on their way over to his last known address right now."

"A serial rapist with a criminal record? How difficult to believe." The captain's sarcasm was obvious.

Jon grabbed the notebook out of his pocket with his notes from Dana Grimaldi. He turned to Zane. "Did the DNA belong to Tony Shefferly?"

Zane stopped midstride, his posture stiffening. "Why do you ask that?"

"That's the victim's ex-boyfriend."

Zane glanced at Captain Harris, then back at Jon. "No, it belonged to Wade Shefferly, Tony's brother."

Chapter Twelve

It had been a long damn day.

Last night Captain Harris still hadn't wanted to admit defeat even when the DNA was discovered as the ex-boyfriend's brother's.

It had taken the man's arrest, hours of questioning through the night and finally unshakable alibis confirmed today for at least three of the other rapes before the captain had admitted Shefferly wasn't the serial rapist they were looking for.

Jon knew after only five minutes of talking to him that he was not smart enough, not controlled enough, not *focused* enough, to be the man responsible for the other attacks.

Shefferly had confessed to what he'd done to Dana Grimaldi. Evidently he'd been angry to the point of hatred at how she'd treated his brother when she cheated on him and broke up with him. He'd thought he could get away with exacting some revenge on his brother's behalf by attack-

ing her in the parking lot. He was hoping the serial rapist would be blamed, although Shefferly
swore he'd never actually planned to rape Dana,
just knock her around and scare her.

Wade Shefferly would be going to jail—*back*
to jail—for what he did to Dana. While Jon was
happy about that, it still meant their rapist was
on the loose.

If frustration in the police department had
been high before Shefferly's arrest, it was twice
as bad now. The force had gotten its hopes up
then dashed.

"I suppose you want to say, 'I told you so,'"
Captain Harris had muttered when Shefferly's
alibi checked out for the other rapes.

Jon didn't want to say, "I told you so." He
didn't want to say anything but "Let's work together and find the bastard responsible before
another woman pays the price."

But he'd been trying to say that since he arrived. Nobody was listening.

Today had been even worse with Jon taking
the full brunt of the detectives' and the captain's frustration. In a case of this magnitude,
with massive media attention, tempers always
flared. People needed somewhere to aim their
vexation; Jon's direction seemed easiest for everyone. After all, he was the one who had been
called in especially for this case. The one who

was supposed to have the expertise needed to get results.

So far, nothing he'd done had been any more useful than anything else.

He knew part of his job as a member of the crisis-management unit was to help the local PD focus its frustration in the right manner, even if it was at him. Damn, if he hadn't had to almost bite his tongue all the way off to keep from snapping back when the men wanted someone to blame.

When Jon had called in to Omega to report the copycat attack and subsequent arrest, his frustration bubbled over. Steve Drackett had tried to assure Jon that Jon was doing everything he could do.

Jon knew he wasn't. He was currently on his way to rectify that.

He needed Sherry.

In his entire professional career Jon couldn't remember ever feeling so torn. He needed Sherry on this case. Her expertise. Her abilities.

He also had a bone-deep need to just be with her, be near her, protect her.

He was afraid he couldn't have both. That if he pushed for one, he couldn't have the other. That if he made a romantic move, and then asked for her help with the case, she might think he was manipulating her to get what he needed.

Jon knew he should put the case first. Ask for her professional help and step back personally.

But as he pulled up in her driveway and saw her open the door and smile at him as he walked up the steps, Jon knew he wouldn't do that.

There was no way he was going to be able to keep his distance from her.

He walked straight up to her and, bending his knees slightly, wrapped both his arms around her waist and hips before straightening to his full height. This brought her neck right up to his face. He buried it in her hair and just breathed.

For the first time all day he felt as though he could actually get air in and out of his lungs without difficulty.

Her arms came around his shoulders and he was thankful—beyond thankful—she didn't pull away. He just needed a minute to clear his head, to be around someone who didn't wish that he would leave town as soon as possible.

Of course, he wasn't even sure that was true with Sherry. She probably thought he was nuts, hugging her like this without even saying hello.

Jon forced himself to release her and set her feet down on the floor. He eased back slowly, afraid of what he was going to see on her face when he looked there.

It wasn't the ridicule or scorn he was half expecting. Just shining blue eyes coupled with her beautiful smile.

"Hey," she greeted him, her Texan upbringing evident in the word.

"Sorry about that," Jon responded. "It's been a hell of a day."

"No apology necessary. I know what it's like to need some sort of lifeline."

Jon imagined she did. "Do you have one? Someone who keeps you grounded when you're doing your work for the Bureau?" He was pretty sure he already knew the answer. Not having someone to help anchor her was part of the reason she was suffering to such a degree now.

"No, not really."

"You need someone. A friend, colleague. Someone. Everybody does."

She nodded. "You're right. Trying to do this alone… The darkness can become too heavy."

"Your supervisor at the Bureau should've provided you with a mentor, or an agent or even the contact info of the FBI therapist. Someone for you to talk to."

"Yeah, I think she meant to. Things just happened fast, crazy fast, when I started working for them. I traveled around a lot, to different field offices, so I wasn't around the same people all the time."

"Still…"

"Oh, I agree I needed someone." Her eyebrows gathered in and she started rubbing her hands together in an absent fashion. "I just thought it was me being weak, letting my artistic nature get the better of me, so I didn't tell anyone how much I was struggling, even when they asked."

Jon grabbed her hands to stop the nervous movement. "Even seasoned agents struggle with being bombarded by the worst side of human nature day after day. And they go through training you never had."

"I guess so." Sherry shrugged. "So, bad day for you, huh?"

"How about if I tell you about it over dinner? Or, if you don't want to, we don't have to talk about the case at all. Either way, I didn't get to eat any lunch and I'm starved."

"Sounds great to me."

"Maybe we'll even make it into the restaurant this time."

Jon meant that hopefully they wouldn't be disturbed by another call having to do with the case. But as soon as their eyes met and the heat was flashing between them again, Jon knew they were both thinking of the same thing: that kiss last night.

MAYBE WE'LL EVEN *make it into the restaurant this time.*

It was all Sherry could do not to suggest they skip the restaurant altogether and just stay here at the house. Order pizza, if he was that hungry.

As much as Sherry wanted to explore this heat between them, she wasn't sure that it was the

smart thing to do. Her emotional balance tee-
tered so precariously right now, she wasn't sure
if she could trust her own feelings.

If she was honest, she wasn't 100 percent sure
that Jon wasn't getting close to her just to try to
talk her into helping with the case. She didn't
think he would deliberately set out to seduce
her to get her help or anything like that. But she
knew that getting involved with Jon would be
complicated.

Plus, she'd decided earlier to try to help him
with the case if she could. That is, if she could
without completely losing her sanity.

She didn't want to tell him just yet, hadn't really decided to what degree she was willing to
offer herself. Or to what degree she'd even be
useful if she wasn't able to draw. Offering to help
and then being totally inadequate would be worse
than not offering in the first place.

She'd deal with that as it came. Right now,
dinner. *Not* inside her house. That was too close
to the bed.

"Yes, let's go eat. I'm hungry, too."

In more ways than one.

"The barbecue place okay again?" He looked
as though he might start drooling over the
thought of it, so she wouldn't have had the heart
to say no even if she had wanted to. Not to mention she was born in Texas and there just wasn't
any way she'd say no to barbecue.

"Sure, let me go grab my jacket."

"Are you serious? It's at least eighty-five degrees out here."

"I never know when I'm going to get cold and sometimes the air-conditioning is too cool in places."

He waited on the small porch while she grabbed her lightweight jacket. When she walked back out he was staring at her legs.

"What? Is there something on my skirt?" She hoped not. It was her favorite denim skirt.

"No. I'm just particular to your legs in those boots."

She smiled at him. "Boots are a Texas thing, mostly, I guess."

"We get them in Colorado, but not as much in Colorado Springs where Omega Sector is located. Despite the mountains, that's more a city than anything else."

He opened her car door and she got in, and then he went around and got in himself.

"Are you from Colorado originally?"

"No, born and raised in Cincinnati. Reds, baby, all the way."

She smiled. "That doesn't sound like a football team. You know in Texas, if it's not football, it pretty much doesn't count as a sport."

"This state is officially killing me." He shook his head. "First, everybody at the precinct hates me and now you tell me baseball isn't important."

"Baseball is your thing, huh?"

"Oh, yeah. I got a full ride to college as a pitcher. Was actually hoping to go pro—at least the minors. But I blew out my elbow my junior year."

"I'm sorry. That had to have been difficult."

"Yeah, at the time. But it helped me focus on where I needed to be. It wasn't bad enough to keep me out of the FBI, just bad enough to end my pro dreams. I know I'm doing what I'm supposed to now."

"What do you do exactly? Are you a profiler?"

"That's part of it. I get sent in to crisis situations to help local law enforcement that don't have the resources and/or personnel to handle a situation. I'm the last resort before feds come in and completely take over a case."

"That's why everyone at the precinct hates you?"

Jon smiled as he pulled into the parking lot of the restaurant. "Usually, I'm not very popular the first day or two, but normally my charming personality has won over most of the locals by this stage of the game."

Sherry didn't question that. She had no doubt Jon was good at his job and it didn't take long for most people to see that he was about the case, not power hungry or there to get anybody in trouble.

She also had no doubt he was able to figure out what the locals needed and become that person, to a certain degree. They needed a leader? He could definitely be one. A sounding board? No problem. Source of support? Scapegoat?

"So basically you handle them like you handled me the other day. You figure out what to say to get what you want."

He shot a sideways look at her. "Well, not what *I* want. But, yeah, I guess I'm good at figuring out how to get everyone to work together to solve the case. Get the job done."

Sherry could respect that. Sometimes people needed to be managed, especially with cases like the current one. It didn't make Jon a bad person, but evidently the police department didn't agree with her on that fact.

"The locals are giving you a hard time," she said.

"They're frustrated. We're all frustrated. In their defense, I haven't been able to make any real progress in the nearly ten days I've been here."

Now seemed like a good time to tell him. She just hoped she wasn't making a huge mistake. "Well, I was thinking maybe I could help you. Look over the files and see if there's anything the other artist missed. I'm not promising anything, but I could try."

Chapter Thirteen

The next morning Sherry found herself at the Corpus Christi Police Department. It was the last place she had expected to be on her vacation, but she'd committed, so she was here.

Jon had refused to talk about the case last night during dinner, which had been nice. She'd half expected once she'd agreed to help for him to skip dinner altogether—or maybe hit a fast-food drive-through, since he had missed lunch—and head straight in to work.

But he hadn't. He'd nodded at her offer, parked the car and ushered her inside the little restaurant.

Once they were seated at the booth, she asked, "Aren't you going to start bombarding me with details about the case?"

He looked up from his menu. "Shh. I'm on a date with a very beautiful woman. I don't want to talk about work, lest she think that's the only reason I'm here with her."

"That's not why you're here with me? Are you sure?"

Jon set the menu down. "I'll admit at this point, if a three-year-old came up to me and offered to help I would probably accept it. So, yes, I will gladly accept your help. But, no, that is very definitely not why I am here with you."

The way he looked at her had her heating up again. She was beginning to think if she stuck around him she'd never have to worry about being cold again.

"Okay." She managed not to stammer. "I just wanted you to know that you didn't have to do this just to get me to help."

"I promise I'm not managing you, not handling you. I just want to spend time with you. Tomorrow will be soon enough to start on the case."

Over the next couple of hours they proceeded to eat and drink a couple of beers and just relax. Sherry wasn't sure that she'd ever seen someone eat a meal with as much reverence as Jon ate his brisket. "You must be Texan somewhere in your blood the way you love that sandwich."

"The state is definitely growing on me."

That look again. The heat.

She learned that he was thirty-three years old, had three brothers, and his mom and dad still lived in Ohio. That he'd been married briefly when he was younger until his wife had decided marriage vows just weren't for her and left him for another guy.

"Ouch."

He shrugged. "It was painful at the time, but things happen for a reason. Like baseball not working out, my marriage falling apart helped point me in the direction of Omega Sector. I've never doubted that was where I was supposed to be. Was recruited there straight out of Quantico."

He told her more about his life with Omega; some funny stories about some of his friends and how he'd played a part in cracking open the Chicago terrorist bombing a few weeks ago, which had led to the arrest of a US senator.

She told him about growing up as an only child. Of the parents she wasn't very close to and how she had become a forensic artist.

"One of my friends witnessed a hit and run a couple of years ago in Dallas. She got a good look at the driver but was having a hard time describing him to the police accurately. I worked with her and was able to bring the drawing in, which eventually led to his arrest."

"How'd you end up working for the FBI?"

"Someone from the local field office happened to be there when I came in. They saw what I'd done and asked if I could help with a kidnapping case they were working on. For the first couple of months I only worked a few hours a week."

"Then once they discovered how good you were, you suddenly found yourself there full-time."

She shrugged. "Basically. More than full-time."

"And you probably didn't take a break at all for the past two years, did you? A vacation?"

"No. There wasn't time. There was always a case. Helping stop a kidnapper or a rapist or a robber always seemed more important than a vacation."

"Then your mind decided you'd had enough and the stress triggers started." He got quiet for a long moment before continuing. "Then you did finally take a vacation, but along came someone else needing you to help with a case."

"It's okay," she murmured.

He then moved the conversation back to more neutral topics. More stories of his brothers and friends at Omega that kept her entertained.

All in all, it was a thoroughly enjoyable evening. When he took her home the heat between them—which had nothing to do with the temperature outside—was palpable. Sherry thought she had some big decisions to make when Jon walked her up to her door.

He cupped her face with both hands and slid his fingers into her hair at the nape of her neck, tilting her head back so they were looking at each other.

In that moment, whatever he wanted, she was

willing. She couldn't remember ever wanting something as much as she wanted Jon right then. As his lips moved toward hers, she raised herself up on her toes to meet him.

But instead of the heat-infused kiss she had expected, like the one from yesterday and the one that had been building between them the entire evening, his lips just briefly, softly, touched hers. Then skimmed over to her cheek.

"I had a wonderful time, Texas," he whispered in her ear. "I'll see you tomorrow."

Then he was gone, leaving Sherry to wonder exactly what had happened.

She was still trying to figure that out now as she was directed back to the desk where Jon could be located here at the station.

He wasn't kidding when he said they didn't like him. Even the uniformed officers working the front desk had sneered when she said who she was here to see. She could see why that would wear thin pretty quickly.

He smiled and stood as she got to the desk the department had assigned him.

"You're like the little wizard who lived under the stairs," she muttered as he pulled up a chair for her to sit in.

"Did I mention that the department was hugely excited that federal law enforcement had been called in to help with the case?"

"They weren't real subtle in demonstrating their disapproval, were they? I guess they couldn't find an actual closet to put you in?"

Jon chuckled. "It's fine. I haven't been here very often anyway. I'm out at scenes and interviews more."

Zane Wales came over to Jon's desk.

"We've got one of the conference rooms cleared so y'all can use it," he told them then turned to Sherry. "Both times I've seen you I've been in a huge hurry. Sorry about that. I'm Zane Wales."

Sherry shook his outstretched hand.

"You're Caroline's…" Sherry wasn't sure what the word was. Friend? Ex-friend? Soul mate? Sworn enemy? Better to stick with something safe. "You know Caroline."

Some emotion flashed across his face too quickly for Sherry to read. Whatever Zane felt for Caroline, it wasn't neutral.

"I do know her. We've known each other since we were in fourth grade."

Evidently, Caroline hadn't been lying when she'd said it was complicated.

They followed Zane into the conference room and Jon set out the files on the table for her.

"I thought you were a forensic artist, not an agent," Zane said.

"She is, but she's just going to look through the files, see if she notices anything we've missed.

At this point, any other qualified set of eyes can only help us."

"I don't disagree with you, but the captain and Spangler will throw a hissy fit if they see her in here."

"This is my call, and I stand behind it. Plus, she's a licensed forensic artist in Texas, so neither of them should have cause for complaint."

"That doesn't mean they won't, though," the younger man said.

"Zane, run some interference for us, man." Jon turned to face him. "Let's all start working like we're on the same team. Because since Dana Grimaldi ended up not being attacked by our guy…"

"He's going to strike again soon," Zane finished for him.

Jon nodded. "If everyone here wants to hate me, that's fine. I can take it. But let's catch this son of a bitch before some other poor woman gets raped."

Zane looked at Sherry and then Jon as he walked to the door. "I'll do what I can. I sure as hell hope you two find something."

"We don't have to do this here if it's going to make everyone mad," Sherry said after Zane left. "I'm not trying to make things worse for you."

"No, I'd rather be here in case there are other resources we need." He walked over to shut the door of the conference room. "Don't worry about anybody else. How do you want to do this?"

She looked at the files, knew the graphic violence she would find when she opened them. Now that it was just the cases sitting right in front of her, Sherry could feel her stomach start to roll, muscles start to tighten. She wanted to turn and walk back out the way she came. Do anything but open these files.

She could feel the chill starting to work its way throughout her body.

She'd made a mistake. She thought she could be of help, thought she could—

"Sherry, look at me."

She couldn't seem to force her eyes away from the documents, from the shattered lives she knew she would find inside.

"Look at me, right now."

Sherry forced her eyes up from the brown folders that had seemed to mesmerize her.

Jon made his way around the table and put both hands on her arms, rubbing them up and down. "I'm going to go through all those files before you even open them. All you need to read is the interview that the other forensic artist had with the victim. You don't need to look at the pictures, don't need the other details. Just the interviews to see if there were any questions you might have asked that were missed."

Jon's hazel eyes were close to hers and she could feel warmth where he was touching her.

"I'm going to be right here, okay?" he said. "Your lifeline, like we talked about yesterday. Everybody needs one in this line of work."

Her lifeline. Yes, she needed someone to make sure she wasn't going under. Jon would do that.

As if he could read her mind he said, "I'll be right here. I won't let you go under."

Sherry took a breath and nodded. Okay, she could do this. At least she would try.

"I'm okay."

He kissed her on the forehead. "You're more than okay. You can do this."

"I hope so."

Chapter Fourteen

He'd almost lost her before they even got started.

It hadn't been hard to see her panic when she saw the files out on the table. Jon could kick himself for not thinking it through more carefully. He should've known he couldn't just hand her the documents—complete with gruesome pictures taken after the victims arrived at the hospital—and expect her to just sort through them.

That would be difficult enough for someone not already dealing with a trauma disorder. Sherry most definitely wasn't ready for that. Jon, like her supervisor at the FBI, had treated her as if she were a trained agent.

She wasn't. She was an artist. She might not have any sort of quirky artistic temperament or behavior, but she still wasn't a trained agent. Everybody, including him, needed to remember that if they wanted Sherry to be able to continue to work long term.

He'd caught it in time and, as he'd promised,

he would continue to be her lifeline throughout this entire process. To keep her from going under when the darkness was too overwhelming.

Sometimes the job of lifeline wasn't sexy. As now. He'd just sat next to her, within arm's reach, as she went through the interviews in the files. Even though the pictures were now gone, the words themselves, the descriptions of the attacks, were bad enough. Especially for someone who had a gift for visualizing.

They'd been at it all day. She was thorough. Taking notes—pages' worth. Asking questions. Jon was so familiar with the cases he could answer most of her questions without even having to reference other materials.

He could tell when it would become overwhelming to her because she would look up for him, almost as if checking to be sure he was still there. When she would see him, she was able to mentally regroup and get back to work.

But it was painful for her.

He'd wanted to stop it, to give her a break, but except for the brief lunch they'd had, consisting of a sub sandwich he'd ordered in from around the corner, she'd wanted to keep going.

A couple of times he'd forced her to stop. To get up, to stretch, to walk around outside and get some sun. Her work ethic was impressive, but Jon was sure it had gone a long way toward the fragile mental state she was in. She had to learn not to labor herself into physical and emotional exhaustion every time she did forensic work.

As much as he wanted her expertise on the case, he also wanted to stop her and pull her into his lap. He was still trying to figure out why— and for heaven's sake *how*—he'd walked away from her last night. All he'd wanted to do was to stay and give in to the heat that had been dancing between them all night.

Every part of him had wanted to remain. Sensing she'd wanted him to stay had made it twice as hard. No pun intended.

But somewhere Jon had known if he wanted to have any chance of a real relationship with Sherry he could not let the physical side of their connection get out of hand too fast. The blend of their personal and professional relationships was just too entwined right now. If he had taken her inside—taken her to bed—as he'd so desperately wanted to do last night, somewhere in the back of her mind his motive would always have been in question.

He didn't let himself dwell too much on the *real relationship* thoughts that were running through his head because, yeah, that was a little scary, since they had known each other for only a few days and had only really kissed once.

Jon knew himself well enough to know that there was nothing casual in what he was feeling for Sherry. He hadn't felt this way since... Hell, he didn't know if he had ever felt this way about a woman.

But right now she needed him professionally. Her trust in him was humbling and he planned to show her that working on cases under the right circumstances and with someone looking out for her well-being didn't have to be traumatic.

And as her lifeline he realized he needed to reel her in.

"Hey, it's time to call it a day." He reached for the file in her hand and was a little surprised when she let it go. Until he realized she was reaching for another one.

"I just want to go back over something that was written about the second victim."

He took that one out of her hand, too. "And you can. Tomorrow."

"Jon, I feel like I haven't made any progress at all. All I've done all day is sit here and read."

"And make about twelve pages of notes. And ask questions and understand more about the case and the monster who's doing this."

She grimaced. "Yeah, but that doesn't do anything to stop him."

"It might do more than you think."

"This isn't the usual way I'm brought into cases. I don't normally look at files at all, especially not before talking to the victims. So I'm probably much slower at processing this stuff than what you're used to."

He ran a gentle hand down her arm. "You're doing fine. I definitely don't expect you to treat this like you're an agent. I'm just hoping that easing you into it this way might help you with your panic attacks if and when you're ready to talk to any of the victims."

Or, God forbid, if there was a new victim that needed to be interviewed.

"I think a couple of these women might actually know more than they think they do," she said. "There're some questions that could've been asked that might help shed some light. I don't know if they were asked or not."

"Like what?"

"Well, I know they didn't see the attacker's features, but they may remember his general size, how broad he was across the chest and shoulders, giving us an idea about his weight, for example."

"That would be at least something."

"I know it doesn't necessarily help you identify the man specifically, but it could at least eliminate certain groups."

"I agree. And at this point we'll take anything."

"The only good thing about having so many victims is that I can try to use their memories as a collective. Nobody has to have seen everything about the guy who attacked them, but maybe they've all seen enough pieces to give us a framework of the whole."

She paused for a moment. "I'll need to talk

to them, Jon." The hesitancy in her voice was evident.

"We can take it slow. Ease you into it."

"We can't take it that slow. You and I both know that."

"Well, I'm not going to let you become an indirect victim. You can only do what you can do, Sherry. I don't expect more than that. Nobody expects more than that."

She looked down at her hands and her hair fell on either side of her face. "I don't even know if I can draw."

He crouched next to her chair. "Like I said, whatever you can do. No matter what, I will be right there with you."

"I'll try." She sighed. "These women have been through so much more than me that I feel like an utter fake even talking as though my problems are important. Line up the interviews as soon as you can."

"Your issues aren't fake, Sherry. And they need to be taken seriously."

She peeked out at him. "You have to admit they're not as serious as the problems these women are facing."

"All that matters is how you handle them. You're trying. That's enough."

She just shrugged.

"But right now we're done for the day." He began putting the files back in the correct order, making sure everything was where it belonged. Sherry stood and began helping him.

"Let's get some dinner, okay?"

"Sure. Can you give me a ride? I caught one with Caroline this morning so I wouldn't have to park."

"It would be my pleasure."

Walking out of the station, Jon could feel eyes on them. Sherry was being branded an outsider merely by her association with him. She didn't seem to notice, or if she did, she didn't care.

Zane had done a good job of keeping the conference room clear today, but when Jon saw Frank Spangler making his way toward them, he knew they weren't going to make it out of the building without a confrontation.

"You may do things differently in your federal job, but here we don't tend to invite our girlfriends to see evidence," Spangler scoffed, stopping their walk toward the main door.

"Spangler, this is Sherry Mitchell. She's assisting us with the serial rapist case." He glanced at Sherry. "Sherry, you remember Spangler?"

Sherry's eyes were cold. "We didn't actually meet, but, yes, I remember you from the other night at the hospital," she said to the older man.

Spangler shifted his weight. "Yeah, well, there isn't much I can do when these women are hysterical."

Sherry took a step toward Spangler, looking

as if she might take a swing at him. Although Jon would do nothing but applaud that action, he knew it would just cause them all a bunch of headache in the long run. He slipped an arm around Sherry's waist, lightly restraining her.

"Spangler has been removed from having contact with any of the victims, since his questioning style doesn't seem to be producing any results," Jon said.

The other man's face turned an odd shade of red. "Nobody could get any results from those women. Not a single one of them saw anything or is willing to even try to remember. I'd like to see you do any better."

Jon felt Sherry look over at him and he tightened his grip on her waist before turning back to Spangler. "Sherry's already done better. After talking to one of the victims only once, she was able to help her remember something she saw."

"Beginner's luck," Spangler snorted.

Sherry stepped away from Jon's arm, closer to Spangler. "I'm not a beginner and I stand by my track record. As you will have to stand by yours, whatever that is." Her voice didn't rise, but her shoulders straightened, which made her almost the same height as Spangler. "I don't need to have decades of experience to know that belittling a woman who has just been horribly assaulted is not only bad police work, but would make me a bad person in general. I'm sorry you're near retirement and *still* haven't figured that out."

She turned from both of them and began walking down the hallway toward the exit.

Jon had to force himself not to laugh out loud at the look on Spangler's face. He shrugged at the older man and turned to chase after Sherry, catching her after just a few steps.

"Way to let him have it," he said.

She balled one hand up into a fist. "I was afraid I was going to punch him. What an utter jackass."

He took her fist and began rubbing the knuckles, smiling. "Well, I'm pretty sure your words had a bigger impact than your fist would have. He would've just had you arrested for assaulting an officer."

"Hey, you guys." Zane Wales walked over to them, a file in hand. "I just wanted to give you an update on the tattoo drawing you provided."

"Anything interesting?" Jon asked.

"It's not gang related, at least not of any gang we know of. We're checking local tattoo shops to see if anyone happens to remember doing any tattoos like this. Unfortunately there're so many places in Mexico someone can go to get ink, it may not have been someone local."

"Okay," Jon said. "Thanks for letting us know."

"This is at least progress," Zane said, turning to Sherry. "It's the first breakthrough we've had at all. Thank you for working with the victim."

Sherry nodded. "I'm glad I could help at least that little bit."

Zane tilted his head in the direction of where they'd just had their discussion with Spangler. "You both should watch your back. Spangler is not going to take very well to the comeuppance you just gave him in front of everyone."

"He started it," Sherry said.

"Yeah, but he won't see it that way," Zane said then looked at Jon. "He's close to retirement, and I was protecting him the other day by not confirming what really happened. That probably wasn't the right call, and I'm sorry."

Jon shrugged. "These are your people. Believe it or not, I do understand that. My job here is not to insinuate that the department is inept. My sole purpose is to help you catch this rapist."

"Yeah, I'm beginning to see that. Hopefully the rest of the team will come around soon, too." He grimaced. "But Spangler won't. Especially not now. So be careful."

"Spangler isn't going to be the one who cracks open this case," Jon said to the younger man.

Zane nodded. "I'll get right on this tattoo."

"Sherry's going to be interviewing the victims again over the next couple of days to see if there's anything she can get that was missed before." Jon didn't assign blame. Perhaps there wasn't anything Spangler missed.

"Okay. I wouldn't announce that to Spangler

or the captain, for that matter." Zane shrugged. "Easier to ask forgiveness than permission in this situation."

Jon chuckled. "Well, I don't need their permission, but I agree with you. We'll have to use the station, but we'll keep this to ourselves as much as possible."

"Sounds good." Zane turned to Sherry and touched the brim of the cowboy hat always on his head. "Ma'am."

Sherry smiled at him.

Damn it, Jon was going to have to get one of those blasted hats if it meant Sherry would smile at him like that.

She turned to him. "What?"

"Nothing," he muttered. Damn cowboy hats.

A couple of hours later after taking her to another of his newfound favorite places to eat—Sherry laughingly telling him that she was glad he had made friends with the waitresses, since he definitely hadn't made any friends in the police department—Jon drove her back to her place. A storm had come up, so he drove slowly through the rain.

Out of the station, both of them had relaxed and just enjoyed each other's company. The more he was around Sherry, the more he wanted to be around her.

But, damn it, he knew this still wasn't the time. Their working relationship was too new.

She needed to know she could trust him to look out for her best interests professionally while they were working on this case.

He rushed around and opened the car door for her and quickly walked her up the steps to her door, covered by a small awning.

"I'll come by and get you tomorrow morning, okay? I've got a call in to victim number one to see if she can come in first thing tomorrow."

She looked at him for a long time as if she was searching for something. Thunder finally crashed and she looked away.

"That's fine," Sherry murmured, unlocking her door and opening it.

Her look—whatever it was, he couldn't quite figure it out—concerned him. "You okay? Nervous about tomorrow? I know it's daunting, but I'm going to be there with you one hundred percent of the—"

His words were cut off by Sherry's lips against his.

A few seconds later he couldn't think of words at all. Could only give in to the heat between them.

She smelled impossibly good.

She tasted even better.

Jon tended to be the one who took the lead in almost all aspects of his life, sexual pursuits included, but he had no problem leaning back against the door frame as Sherry pushed him there. His hands encircled her hips and brought her up close to him. He groaned as she wrapped her arms around his neck, fisting his hair in her hands. They were drowning in the kiss.

Using every ounce of mental energy he had, Jon eased back just slightly. He wanted to make sure she knew he wasn't using her. "Sherry, I just want to make sure—"

"Jon," she murmured against his mouth. "Shut. Up. You think too much. Just kiss me."

It was all the permission Jon needed. He spun them around so that she was flat against the door frame, cupped her face with both hands and took possession of her mouth. Fire ignited as he stroked his tongue against hers.

Both of them moaned, straining to bring their bodies closer together.

Jon reached down and wrapped his arms around her hips, picking her up without breaking the kiss. He walked them through the door, kicking it closed behind them.

He didn't know where her bed was, and didn't care. The farthest he was going to make it was the couch five feet away. He lowered them both down, loving the feel of her arms and legs wrapped around him.

The storm raged on in the distance, second only to the storm of passion between them.

Chapter Fifteen

Sherry woke up warm for the first time in as long as she could remember.

Not just warm. Hot.

That was perhaps because of the very large man wrapped nearly all the way around her, his chest to her back. One of his arms was stretched out under her neck, between her shoulder and the pillow, and the other was tucked around her waist, keeping her close to him. They had slept that way all night.

At least they had once they'd made it to the bed, *finally*, hours later than they'd arrived on the couch.

Sherry was never going to be able to look at the couch again the same way. Heck, she was never going to be able to look at the bed the same way, either. She was glad she was the only one who ever used this house. Even though they owned it, her parents hadn't vacationed here since she was a child.

She'd never be able to enter this house again without thinking of Jon Hatton.

Who was now beginning to stir behind her.

"Good morning," he murmured as he nuzzled her neck then bit it gently. Chills that had nothing to do with cold ran through Sherry's body.

"Good morning to you, too," she whispered back.

"As much as I would like to stay here all day with you, we have Tina Wescott coming in at 9:00 a.m."

She turned so she could face him. "I'm still not sure about my drawing ability."

Sherry's biggest fear was that they would bring this poor woman in to the station, ask her to recount all the details of the worst day of her entire life, that she would remember something—some feature or characteristic of her attacker—and that Sherry wouldn't be able to draw it.

He used his thumb to rub her forehead, ease the worry lines between her brows. "You drew me on the beach the other day."

"Yeah, but that was different. I wasn't thinking about it."

"Either way, the drawing ability is still there. You haven't lost it. You've just got to figure out how to harness that part of your mind and shut out the other."

Sherry nodded, but she had no idea how to do that.

"We'll just take it one minute at a time. Try not to concentrate on the big picture, literally and figuratively, just on what you're doing at that very minute."

It was good advice and similar to the advice she had given herself before. "Baby steps."

"Exactly." He kissed her. "Now let's go out and get some breakfast so we can get to the station on time."

"Okay, I'm going to take a shower." She got out of bed and headed toward the bathroom. "Someone has kept me in bed, participating in naughty deeds all night." She giggled as his hand streaked out and smacked her on the bottom.

"Wasn't just on the bed," he murmured.

In the bathroom her smiled faded. She turned on the shower, then turned and looked at herself in the mirror, leaning her hands on the bathroom counter. She really was afraid of failing. Failing Jon, failing the victim, failing herself.

The bathroom door opened and Jon came to stand behind her. He kissed the top of her shoulder, looking at her in the mirror.

"Whatever happens, we'll get through it together," he whispered in her ear.

"Okay."

"Right now, a shower."

"Only if you'll join me." She smiled at him, turning around.

"What about breakfast? I want to make sure you have the energy you need."

She put a hand on his chest, walking forward and backing him toward the shower. "I'll eat a huge bowl of cereal."

He reached behind him and opened the shower door. Steam flooded around them. "As long as it's healthy cereal," he said as he pulled her up against him hard.

Every thought in her head seemed to vanish as he moved them both under the hot spray of the shower. As he'd said, she'd just take it one minute at a time. This minute especially.

"FOR THE RECORD, those Sugar-O's do not count as healthy cereal," Jon said as they sat in the Corpus Christi interview room an hour later, waiting for Tina Wescott to arrive.

"I was afraid you would stop if I told you what it was," she whispered.

"Honey, I had you naked in a steamy shower. You could've told me we were eating snails for breakfast and I wouldn't have stopped."

"Snails probably would've had more nutritional value." Sherry laughed softly.

Jon was glad to see the pinched look leave her face at least for a few moments. Despite the comfortable room temperature, she was huddling into her denim jacket and rubbing her hands as if to encourage circulation.

He sat next to her and took her hands in his. They did feel icy.

"Hey," he said. "Remember, one minute at a time. Baby steps. Just ask questions, don't worry about drawing."

Her sketch pad was sitting in front of them on the table. Jon noticed she hadn't touched it once. He wanted to help her, but drawing wasn't something he could do. Unless he was willing to turn the heat up and sweat everyone else to death, he couldn't help her much with the cold, either.

Tina Wescott entered the room and Jon greeted her and introduced Sherry. He was concerned for just a moment that Sherry wouldn't be able to get it together enough to talk to the other woman but then watched as she mentally pulled herself up by her bootstraps.

"Hi, Tina." Sherry shook her hand. "I'm so sorry we're meeting under these circumstances."

Tina had been the first person attacked nine weeks ago. For more than a month her rape had been treated as an isolated incident. It was only after the fourth victim that the police department had realized they were dealing with one single attacker.

Sherry made a little small talk with Tina, about the weather, about Texas A&M's lineup for next season's football team—Sherry hadn't been kidding when she'd said Texas was all about football. The two women could talk more intelligently about A&M's offensive line than Jon could talk about most of the pro teams he followed.

They were still talking about the new quarterback who was coming in when there was a knock on the conference room door. Before Jon could even get over to answer it, it opened and Spangler breezed in. Zane Wales entered behind him, his expression apologetic.

"Mind if we sit in?" Spangler asked. "More heads are better than one, right?"

The rapport Sherry had been building with Tina was instantly lost. The last thing Jon wanted to do was to make it worse by having it out with Spangler right there.

Jon looked over at Tina, "Is it okay with you if they stay?"

"Sure." Tina shrugged. "That's fine."

Jon wished she had told them to get lost, but he didn't blame her for wanting all the help she could get. "If at any point you're feeling too crowded, we can definitely thin out the room. Don't be afraid to say something."

"I haven't remembered anything else," Tina told them, looking down at her hands.

"That's fine," Sherry said. "I'm just trying to piece together any little bits you or any of the other women remember. Perhaps together, that can give us a clearer picture of the whole."

"Okay."

"I'm just going to warn the officers in here not

to interrupt. I'm sure that won't be a problem."
She looked pointedly at Frank Spangler.

"I'm just here to observe." He held out his
hands in front of him in a gesture of innocence.

"Great," Sherry said with a smile that didn't
reach her eyes. "Observing doesn't require any
talking. And maybe you'll learn something."

Jon coughed to keep from laughing. Spangler glared at Sherry but didn't say anything,
just crossed his arms and sat back in his seat.
Zane smiled next to the older man, but was sure
not to let him see. Tina didn't seem to notice the
tension at all.

Sherry grabbed her sketch pad and opened it
without hesitating, obviously something she'd
done multiple times before. Good. She was focusing on her annoyance with Spangler, not on
freezing up. He might have come in to try to
make her feel uncomfortable or to intimidate her,
but it was working to her advantage instead.

"Tell me what the weather was like on the day
of your attack," Sherry said softly to Tina.

For the next three hours Jon listened as Sherry
talked to Tina, often asking her questions that
seemed irrelevant. Such as the weather question
she'd started with or questions about what had
been on the radio that day.

Then Jon realized Sherry was attempting to involve as many of Tina's five senses as she could.

Any of them might trigger a memory of something Tina hadn't realized she knew.

Sherry's cognitive interviewing skills matched any Jon had ever seen at Omega Sector or any other law-enforcement group he had worked with. She had a gift. It was easy to see that Tina felt comfortable with her and was willing to answer questions.

Over and over Sherry backed Tina up to about an hour before the attack and had her walk through that time period. It helped Tina's mind to refocus on that day without actually having to concentrate on the attack itself. Then each time Sherry took Tina a little further into the attack, so that she didn't have to describe the entire brutal event all at once.

Baby steps.

Even with Sherry's calm, measured method of asking questions as they got into the heart of Tina's attack, Jon could easily see the toll it was taking on both women. Tina was crying. Sherry was nestling into her jacket.

Although Tina hadn't given her any details to draw, Sherry still had the pencil in her hand. Glancing over at her, he could see her attempt to keep her hand from shaking.

"Okay, Tina, last time, I promise," Sherry said, a slight tremor noticeable. "Let's focus on when you opened the door."

Tina took a shuddery breath. "The doorbell

rang. I was irritated because I couldn't find the remote to pause my TV show. I was trying to hurry. That's why I didn't check the window, like I normally would have."

"That's right. I'm sure that's true," Sherry assured her, trying to keep her focused on the memory itself rather than what she could've done differently.

"I was still listening to the show as I opened the door, so I wouldn't miss anything." More tears flowed down Tina's face. Zane slid a box of tissues to within her reach in case she wanted them. "When the door was ajar just a crack, he slammed it all the way open. I stumbled back a step and he hit me."

Tina began crying in earnest.

"Okay, I want you to stop there, Tina." Sherry reached out and touched the other woman's arm. "Right before he hit you, were you able to see his face at all?"

"No, I'm sorry." She shook her head. "The sun was too bright behind him. And then he hit me too fast. I'm sorry."

"Tina." Sherry's voice was shaky, difficult to hear over Tina's sobs.

"I got all of this before. Why drag her through this again?" Spangler muttered.

He hated to admit it, but Jon had to agree. They already knew Tina hadn't seen her attacker's face. No matter how good a forensic artist

Sherry was, there was no way she could force Tina to describe something she hadn't seen.

Jon started to interrupt, but Sherry held out an arm to silence him.

Sherry began again with a stronger voice. "Tina, listen to me. I know you didn't see his face. That's okay. That's not what I want to ask you."

Tina was visibly relieved. "It's not?"

"No, what I want you to do is stand up. Freeze in your mind those first few seconds of when your attacker entered your house."

"Stand up right now?" Tina took a deep breath in and blew it back out.

"Yes." Sherry put the sketch pad down and stood with her. "Okay, now think about the man in the doorway. You were about three feet away from the door when he pushed in and struck you the first time, right?"

"Yeah, that would be about right."

"Okay, so concentrate on before he pushed you to the floor. When you were looking at him in the doorway, what angle did you have your neck?"

Tina looked over at Sherry. "I don't understand."

Sherry walked over to Jon and slipped her hand under his arm to get him to stand. Then she brought him to stand about three feet away from Tina.

"See how you have to crane your neck back

to look at Agent Hatton? Was your neck like that?" Sherry went over and grabbed Zane, who was about five-ten, and pulled him around to the other side of the table next to Jon. "Or was it more like looking at Detective Wales?"

Jon realized what Sherry was doing.

"Detective Wales," Tina responded. "Definitely more like Detective Wales."

The men sat. Sherry reached over and squeezed Tina's arm. "That's good. Helpful."

"Really?" Tina looked around the room.

"It lets us know that your attacker was probably around five foot nine or ten," Jon said. "That's good, usable information."

"Thank God." Tina began crying again. "I couldn't stand the thought of being so useless."

Sherry put her arm around her. "The opposite, in fact. Very helpful. I'm going to talk to the other women and we'll continue piecing things together. But that's enough for today. Maybe we can talk again another time."

Tina was obviously exhausted. Zane helped her gather her things and walked her out.

"Why did you stop just when you were getting somewhere?" Spangler asked.

"Knowing when to quit is just as important as knowing when to push," Sherry said as she took her seat. "Memory is a fragile thing. Pushing too hard or for too long can do more damage than good."

"You've got her subconscious thinking down a different path than it was before. She might begin to remember more details," Jon said.

"I hope so," Sherry said. "Because knowing your perp is about average height is not going to help you catch him."

She was withdrawing in her chair, wrapping her arms around her midsection. Sherry had needed a stop to the questioning just as much as Tina had.

"Like you said, it's a detail we didn't have before. We'll just keep adding details together as we get them."

Spangler stood. "Yeah, well, knowing his probable height is not going to stop this guy. So you just put that woman through hell for no reason."

He left shaking his head, Jon and Sherry staring after him.

Chapter Sixteen

Sherry felt a little nauseated, as if she was going to throw up. Was Spangler right? Should she have kept pushing? Had she stopped to spare Tina or to spare herself?

Had she stopped because she knew if Tina did happen to remember something concrete, there was no way Sherry was going to be able to draw it?

Spangler would just have loved that.

"Whatever you're thinking, you need to just cut it out right now." Jon was looking at her from across the conference room table.

"Maybe I should've kept going."

"She'd had enough. Like you said, pushing would've been detrimental."

"Yeah, but I think I actually stopped because pushing would've been detrimental for me, not her."

Jon came around and sat on the edge of the table, his long legs stretched out in front of him, next to her chair. "It would've been detrimental for you both. You made the right call. If you hadn't ended it when you did, I would have."

"I don't trust myself anymore, Jon."

He reached over and rubbed her chin with his thumb. "Baby steps."

Sherry just shrugged. She was afraid baby steps weren't going to get them where they needed to go fast enough.

"Let's get out of this room for a while, okay?" he said.

But out in the detective area where all the desks were visible and everyone seemed to be looking at them, it wasn't any less stressful for Sherry.

"You want to take a walk outside?" she asked. "I need some fresh air." He would never let her walk on her own.

They walked in silence. Sherry appreciated that Jon understood that she just needed some time to pull herself together. The police station was in the more industrial, less touristy, side of town, so it wasn't as nice as walking on the beach, but at least it was quiet.

Last night's storm seemed to have broken the heat wave. It was cooler, in the low eighties, more traditional for weather in June here. The air was muggy, full of the rain from the past few hours.

At first breathing the outside air—even as muggy as it was—was exactly what Sherry needed. Jon's presence in the conference room had done a pretty good job of keeping the cold away, but the last of the chill was vanquished by the coastal heat.

After walking awhile, Sherry started to get the feeling—as she had a few days before when walking to Jasmine Houze's house—that someone was watching her. She stopped and turned but, like then, didn't see anything out of the ordinary.

"What's wrong?" he asked.

Sherry shook her head. "Nothing."

"Not nothing. You were doing okay and then you got all weirded out."

"I just felt like someone was watching us," she said.

"I didn't see anything or anyone out of place."

"I know. It's just me. This happened a couple of days ago, too, when I was walking to Jasmine's house. Plus, I also felt like everyone was staring at me at the police station." She sighed out loud. "I'm pretty sure these are signs I am either losing my grip on reality or that I am just really, really self-involved."

Jon put his arm around her. "Well, I can officially attest that neither is correct."

"Yeah, I'm not so sure about that."

They turned to work their way back to the station. Sherry wasn't surprised when Jon made her stop at one of the hole-in-the-wall barbecue joints. The man loved his food. Maybe she couldn't make him stay in Texas, but brisket probably could.

Where in the world had that thought come from?

Despite last night, there had been no talk of a relationship—long-or short-term—between them. Sherry assumed Jon would be heading back to Omega headquarters in Colorado once this was over. She'd be staying here, or at least returning to Houston.

The thought didn't sit well with Sherry. She refused to force the "we need to talk about our relationship and where it's going" conversation after only one night with him.

That was one thing she would just have to let happen on its own accord. She had enough on her mind without worrying about their relationship. It would have to be discussed later.

Back at the station, sitting at Jon's desk, looking over the notes she had taken from this morning's talk with Tina, Sherry could feel eyes watching her again. She'd like to draw a picture of the man in the doorway whom Tina had described—even with all the blanks. But the negative looks from almost every direction were damaging her calm. Her calm was pretty damn precarious to begin with.

At least this time she wasn't the only one who noticed it.

"You guys are the talk of the entire building," Zane said as he came over to give Jon a file.

Jon just shrugged. "What's new? They've been shooting daggers at me since day one."

"Yeah, well, Spangler is telling everyone who will listen that you're putting these women through unnecessary hardship—his words, exactly—by bringing them in again to talk to Sherry."

Sherry met Jon's eyes across the desk. Jon shook his head before looking back at Zane.

"He's arguing that Sherry doesn't have the expertise to be working a case of this magnitude. That you brought her here because the two of you are romantically involved."

Sherry's eyes flew to Jon's again. Again, he gave a tiny shake of his head.

"Well, Spangler is an idiot. Because first, Sherry has an impeccable record with the Bureau over the past two years and it will stand up to any scrutiny. And second, my idea of romancing a woman does not involve me bringing her in to talk to people who have been sexually assaulted."

"I pretty much argued those two points with him. So now I'm not on the popular side, either." Zane shrugged.

"If I didn't know better, I would almost think that Spangler is deliberately stalling this case."

Zane shook his head. "I don't think he is. He's

just used to being the head honcho around here. Giving up the glory on the last big case before his retirement doesn't sit well with him."

"He can keep all the glory," Sherry said. "I don't want any of it."

"Neither do I," Jon agreed. "I don't care who takes the credit. I just want this bastard caught."

"Spangler is not such a bad guy. He'll come around."

Sherry wasn't so sure.

"I didn't have any luck with tattoo artists in the area," Zane continued. "I've got some men taking the picture around to more shops farther out of the immediate vicinity. I also took it by the hospital this morning to show Nurse Carreker and some of the other staff and EMTs just before coming here."

"Good, you never know when that will net some results. Nurse Carreker runs a tight ship."

Sherry looked at Zane, who nodded at her before looking down to ardently study the file in his hand. Interesting that he had gone to the hospital to show the tattoo drawing just as Caroline was likely to be arriving to clock in for her shift.

Sherry decided not to bring up that point. Neither Zane nor Caroline ever seemed to want to discuss Zane and Caroline.

"I've got to meet with the captain and the mayor for a couple of hours," Jon said after Zane promised to keep them informed if he heard anything and left. "You want me to take you home or do you want to stay here?"

Really, Sherry didn't want to do either. The thought of sitting at her house alone wasn't appealing, especially given the story she'd just heard over and over from Tina. But staying here at the station without Jon around wasn't particularly tempting, either.

"I don't guess I can talk you into letting me walk on the beach while you're in your meeting."

"Alone?"

Sherry almost giggled at the way his eyebrows raised so high.

"Uh, no," he said.

"I don't want to stay here, Jon. There's enough staring with you here. I'm not sure what will happen with you gone."

"I can ask Zane if he can hang around. Just run interference."

"I don't need to be babysat. Zane has other stuff he needs to do."

"I'm sorry I can't cancel this meeting. It's about strategy with the press. Keeping people calm right now is one of the best things we can do. Law enforcement is going to become a lot more difficult if people start trying to take things into their own hands or see an attacker in any person who looks at them wrong."

The city had been on the verge of panic for the past few weeks. Jon's expertise in this area was probably as critical for the case as Sherry's was with the victims.

"How about if I go over to the hospital? There's a nice outdoor sitting area with some gazebos. Public yet quiet. Lots of people around but not any who will bother me."

The hospital was only a couple of blocks away.

"Okay, I'll walk you," Jon said. "Promise me you'll stay there. No walking alone."

"Promise."

HAVING SOMETHING GO right was a nice change of pace in the case. Jon left Mayor Birchwood's office feeling as though for the first time in the nearly two weeks he had been here, someone had actually listened to him.

Working the press in a case like this was just as important as the police work. The city was on the verge of panic and it was now up to the mayor to keep that from happening.

Captain Harris had tried to skew information to make Jon look incompetent, but fortunately the mayor wasn't interested in any sort of imagined rivalry between local and federal law enforcement. He just wanted what was best for his city.

When the captain realized Birchwood wasn't looking for a scapegoat, the three of them were able to work as a team to come up with a media plan as well as to discuss the case and what was happening with the investigation.

Either Spangler hadn't gotten to the captain with his opinion about Sherry yet or the captain felt it wasn't in his best interest to bring it up. He hadn't interrupted when Jon talked about her and what they'd discovered so far about the general height of the attacker and the tattoo.

The mayor had asked for Jon's advice about the statement he was giving on live television tonight. Jon had encouraged him to ask the public to maintain common sense, caution and safety in numbers. Not to open the door to anyone unfamiliar.

"Anything else?" Mayor Birchwood had asked.

"I would appeal to the heart of being Texan," Jon replied. "I've been here two weeks and I already see how people here band together. Remind them that they are Texans. They can take the heat. They're strong."

The mayor jotted down some notes. Even Harris nodded.

"Okay, good. Are we looking at people with previous records?" Birchwood asked.

"Always," Captain Harris responded. "As Agent Hatton will attest, it's hard to pin this guy down to specifics."

Jon agreed. "He's very smart. Genius IQ probably. Very controlled. Knows how forensics works and is careful not to leave any traceable evidence behind."

The mayor grunted. "And that other attack? Not the same guy?"

"No, sir," Harris said. "It became evident that he was just using some basic information from media reports of the attack to try to get away with terrorizing his brother's ex-girlfriend."

"I'm glad you were able to distinguish him from the real rapist before we reported that we had made an arrest, only to discover we were wrong. That would've been a major embarrassment."

Jon very decidedly did not look at Captain Harris.

Harris shifted in his chair. "Yes, sir, it was a team effort."

"What about this tattoo?" the mayor asked. "Should we release that to the press?"

Harris and Jon glanced at each other. That was a tough question. Jon deferred to Harris, since it was ultimately his call.

"I think we should wait," Harris said to the mayor. "Only use it if we have no other options."

"You don't think it might help us find the guy?"

"I just think we might get too many people accusing too many other people of possibly being the perpetrator. Vigilante justice could get out of control."

"I agree," Jon said. "The tattoo doesn't seem to be involved with any gang symbols, but that doesn't mean that our guy is the only one out there with it. We don't want people taking the situation into their own hands."

"And he doesn't know we know about it," Harris finished. "That could possibly give us an advantage. Especially in a lineup."

"Should I mention you're working with this Sherry Mitchell?"

Jon didn't want her name out there and he knew Sherry wouldn't want it, either. "Not by name, definitely. But mentioning the department is working with a forensic artist for details beyond just facial features might help put the public a little more at ease."

"All right," Mayor Birchwood said, standing. This meeting was obviously at an end. "Thank you, gentlemen. I know I don't have to say this, but catching the attacker is of utmost importance. The city is balancing precariously right now. Tourist profit margins are down because no one wants to bring their family where there's a door-to-door rapist."

Jon and Harris both nodded. They, more than anybody, knew what was at stake here.

"Please keep my office posted if anything changes." The mayor showed them to the door.

"I hope your new forensic artist can get more information soon," Captain Harris said as they walked down the hall to the elevator. "Everything the mayor said in there was right. The city is going to blow up soon if we don't get a handle on this case."

"If there's information to be had in the victims' minds, Sherry Mitchell will get it."

"That's not what Frank Spangler is saying."

"Spangler is just trying to save face."

"That may be true, but we're still running out of time."

Jon couldn't agree more. After saying good-bye to Captain Harris, he drove to the hospital from city hall.

He could understand about the city being on the borderline of panic. Right now, without Sherry in his sight, even pretty sure that she was safe, Jon could feel the panic licking at his heels.

If everyone in a city of more than half a million people was feeling this sort of stress about the safety of their loved ones, then, yes, the city was very definitely on the verge of a panic attack.

And had the words *loved one* just gone through his mind in conjunction with Sherry?

He would be the first one to admit that he hadn't been able to get her out of his mind from the moment he'd seen her. Last night and this morning had been possibly the best of his life.

But not to get carried away with the feelings. He needed to think this through further. He *always* thought things through before letting his emotions get involved.

Still, he couldn't deny the profound feeling of

rightness, coupled with relief, when he saw her sitting in the courtyard where he'd left her. Safe and looking more relaxed than she had seemed all day.

Well, almost all day. He could think of a time in the shower this morning where she'd definitely been more relaxed.

"What are you grinning about?" she asked as he walked up to her.

"Um…relaxation techniques." He sat next to her, kissing her on the cheek.

"How did your meeting go?"

"Better than I thought it would. Mayor Birchwood is a pretty reasonable guy. He just wants what's best for his city. How about you? Did you get bored?"

"No, Nurse Carreker stopped by for a few minutes. And Dr. Trumpold."

"That really handsome Italian-looking doctor?"

"Yeah." She all but sighed.

Jon rolled his eyes. "And here I thought I was leaving you here to keep you safe from a serial rapist. I should've locked you up in a cell at the station so you couldn't get into any trouble."

She smiled. "We just talked. Don't be jealous."

Jon snorted. "I am not jealous. He's short. I don't know why women would be into him."

"He's brilliant, successful and probably very rich. Besides, everybody's short compared to you, so that doesn't count." She reached over and put both arms around his neck where he sat next to her on the bench. "Don't worry, he's not my type."

"Humph." Jon turned his head and looked up into the distance in mock offense.

Sherry leaned closer. "How about if we go over to my house and I make you dinner, then prove to you just how much more interested I am in federal agents than handsome doctors?"

Jon glanced over at her without moving his head. "I don't know. I might need a lot of convincing."

"I think I'm up to the challenge."

Chapter Seventeen

Sherry sashayed up the steps to her porch, knowing that Jon was watching from the car. They had decided on the way that if he showed up at the station for the third day in a row wearing the same clothes, people were definitely going to notice. He wanted to take her to the condo where he was staying.

They'd agreed they would stop by her house so she could grab whatever she needed to make dinner, and beyond, before going to his place. Jon didn't offer to come in and Sherry didn't insist. They both knew if he followed her into her house they would never make it back out of the bed tonight.

To make up for the damage to Jon's delicate ego after the doctor comment.

Sherry actually laughed out loud. Jon was going to milk that for as much as he could. And she didn't mind at all.

She was still smiling as she grabbed the things

she would need for the meal she planned—fish tacos—and put them in a couple of paper grocery bags by the sink. As she did so she tried to think of the sexiest undergarments she had brought with her on this vacation.

Nothing too spectacular. She definitely hadn't been planning on a romance. But she did have some black lacy things somewhere in her room.

Or maybe she could just change into a sundress and have absolutely nothing on under that.

She rushed from the kitchen into the bedroom, a smile plastered on her face. Jon wouldn't know what hit him.

She smelled it first. Her smile faded as her nostrils were accosted with a metallic scent. Like iron or copper or something rusting.

Had a pipe burst? It was the only thing she could think of that could be rusting.

Her eyes adjusted to the gathering dusk in her bedroom and Sherry saw something on her bed. Oh, no, the roof had leaked during yesterday's storm. She could see the dark stain all over the bed, ruining the quilt. She touched it and was surprised at how oddly thick the water was. And sticky.

She turned the lamp on next to her bed to get a better look and jumped backward, knocking the lamp over but not shattering the bulb.

Blood. It wasn't water, it was *blood*. An obscene amount of it, making a garish stain on her bed's cream-colored quilt.

Right in the middle of it was a note, its white seeming neon against all the red. *Stay out of this.*

Sherry felt she was going to vomit, but she forced it down. Cold descended over her entire body rapidly, uncontrollably. She couldn't stop the shudders that racked her frame; they glued her in place.

Every shadow cast from the setting sun filtering through the window now held a potential enemy. Was the person who did this still in her house?

The thought was enough to jolt her body into taking another step away from the bed.

Jon was right outside. She just had to get him.

She slid her way along the wall with her back to it, eyes glued on the bed. On the blood. So much of it. Once she made it through the door frame of the bedroom, she stumbled as if she were drunk back down the little hall into her kitchen. The iciness in her limbs made movement difficult and violent shivers made her teeth clack together like castanets. Her vision began fading in and out.

She took two steps and leaned heavily on the kitchen island. She saw a bloody handprint there and startled back, until she realized it was from her own hand. Blood, from where she had touched the bed.

Shadows loomed everywhere. She had to get out.

The front door was only a few yards away. She forced her legs to move forward. She had to make it out to Jon. Just a few more steps.

It wasn't safe here.

ONE LOOK AT Sherry's face as she seemed to stumble out the door and Jon knew immediately that something wasn't right. He was out of the car and running up the couple of stairs in seconds.

"What? Sherry, what is it?"

She held up her hand and he felt the air rush out of his lungs as he saw the blood.

"Did you cut yourself? Are you okay?" He looked at her hand but couldn't see any wound on it, only mostly dried blood.

He supported her arms as she grasped his shirt, nearly falling on him. Up close he could see she was paper white, her skin cold to the touch.

"Are you hurt, Sherry? Talk to me, baby."

"N-no." Her teeth were chattering so badly she could barely get the word out. "In…inside."

Jon pulled his Glock out of the holster and turned to face the door, sweeping Sherry behind his back so he was between her and whatever had terrorized her in such a way. "Is someone in there?"

"I don't know." She grasped the back of his shirt to keep him from going forward.

"I'm just going in to check, make sure we're safe. Stay right here, okay? If anyone comes out here, you scream your head off."

Jon didn't want to leave her, but he needed to know what was inside and if it was a threat to them. He turned around and glanced at Sherry.

She nodded. "Bedroom." The word was barely a whisper.

Jon entered the house cautiously, checking all rooms and closets on his way in. He examined all other rooms in the small single-story house before going to the master bedroom.

He saw the blood on the bed immediately. It was impossible to miss, even with the lamp turned over on the floor. But he secured the bathroom and walk-in closet before turning to give the room his full attention.

Confident the house was empty, he returned his Glock to its holster and walked closer to the bed.

The curse that flew out of his mouth was vile at the sight of the blood covering the bed he and Sherry had spent so many hours on the night before. Viler still when he saw the note lying pristine white in the center of the mess.

Stay out of this.

There was no doubt in his mind what that meant. Rage, and not just a little bit of fear, flew through him at the thought of this monster turning his attention to Sherry.

Jon pulled his cell phone out of his pocket and dialed Zane Wales. "It's Hatton," he said without preamble. "I need uniformed officers and a full forensic team out at Sherry Mitchell's place right damn now."

"Oh, my God, Jon. Please tell me—"

"No, she wasn't attacked." Jon cut him off, not wanting to allow the other man to think the absolute worst. "But her house was visited by him." He gave Zane the address.

He could hear Zane firing off commands to whoever was nearby.

"Not that I don't believe you, but how do you know it was him?"

"He left her a note."

Zane gave an angry curse similar to Jon's. "Do you need an ambulance?"

"No, no one's hurt. At least not at the scene. Just hurry up and get here. Thanks, Zane." He disconnected the call.

Jon was thankful there was no body lying in Sherry's house, but he knew that much blood—if it was from a single person—would definitely mean there was a body somewhere.

It looked as though their rapist might just have escalated to murderer.

Jon didn't touch anything, knowing Forensics could get more from a clean scene than he could get from disturbing it.

Besides, he needed to get back out to Sherry.

She was still on the small portico, huddled down on the ground now instead of standing. Her arms were wrapped around her head as she rocked herself back and forth.

"Sherry, sweetheart." Jon crouched next to her and pulled her into his arms. "It's okay."

He heard her take a shuddery breath, but she didn't look up.

"Is anyone in there?"

"No, the house is empty."

"Is there a bod—" She stopped to take another shaky breath and get though the word. "A body?"

"No, there's no body anywhere in the house. I searched."

She nodded slightly. "But all that blood…"

He pulled her in tighter. "It definitely came from somewhere, but the body is not here. That much I can assure you."

She didn't say anything for a long time, but at least she let go of her head and rested against him. Jon knew the police officers would be here any moment, but he didn't care. There was no way he was letting go of Sherry while she still needed him. Even if they were blocking the door. They could step over them to get inside.

"Did you see the note?" Sherry's voice was tight, hoarse.

Jon kissed the top of her head. "Yes."

"It's him and he knows I'm working with you." Her shaking was coming back.

"Hey, listen to me." He reached down and tilted her chin up with a finger. "Nothing is going to happen to you. I will be with you every minute until we catch this guy. Or if I can't be, I will make sure someone who we can trust is."

He could tell she was still working things through her mind. And it would get worse before it got better. Her home, her safety, had been violated. It would take time for her to come to grips with everything going on.

But what Jon told her was the truth. He was determined to make sure she was safe.

"Do you think we could get you over to my car?" he asked her as he saw blue lights flashing in the distance. "Police are going to be here soon. Forensics. A lot of people going in and out. You might feel better if you're not right here in the door."

She nodded. "Okay. And I can help inside."

"No, absolutely not." There was no way in hell he was letting her back in there, even if there was something she could do, which there wasn't. He gentled his tone. "We need to let the forensic techs do their job. You and I both need to stay out of the way as much as possible."

Actually, Jon planned to be there. He would make sure he didn't contaminate any of the evidence, but he was going to make damn sure this was being handled correctly. Sherry didn't need to experience the scene again. He was quite sure it would already be burned into her mind for a long time.

"Let's get you over to my car." He helped her stand. Her skin was still rough with chills.

"I need to wash my hands," she whispered. "I got blood on your shirt."

He hugged her to him. "Don't worry about that, baby. And I'll get something for you to wipe your hands with until we can get you back to my place and you can take a shower."

She didn't give him any trouble about that, for which he was thankful. She was going to stay where he could protect her himself.

He walked her slowly over to his car and opened the door, easing her in. The uniformed officers were parking and he motioned to them to hold their position.

He grabbed his jacket from the backseat and wrapped it around her. "You stay right here, okay? I'm going to help coordinate what's going on inside, but I'm going to leave a uniformed officer right outside the door."

Sherry nodded, though her eyes were unfocused, staring straight ahead. Being somewhat in shock was understandable.

He knelt next to her so they could see eye to eye. "Hey." He brushed back a strand of hair from her face. "You hang in there, okay? I'll be back as soon as I can and we'll get out of here."

Her eyes focused on him and she nodded. He kissed her forehead.

He stood and closed the door. The sooner he got this finished, the sooner he could get back to Sherry. Jon motioned over two of the uniformed police officers who had showed up.

"You two are both to stay here, do you understand?"

The young officers, one male and one female, both nodded, although neither looked happy about it.

"This is Sherry Mitchell. This is her house. What's in there is pretty horrific and she stumbled onto it unawares. She's in shock, and more than that she's a possible target of the serial rapist."

They were taking the situation much more seriously now.

"I want both of you here, guarding this car, the entire time. If one of you needs to leave, you send someone to get me first. No one, under any circumstances, is to take Ms. Mitchell anywhere, except me."

As he walked away he turned back. "Have someone get her some water. And something to wipe the blood off her hands."

Zane had showed up and walked over to him. They made their way to the front door together.

"What the hell, man?" Zane said in way of greeting. "What is going on?"

They stepped out of the way so the forensic team could get by with its gear, but followed right behind them. Jon pointed them in the right direction once inside the house. "Our rapist stopped by. Evidently he's not too excited about Sherry working with us."

When they stepped into the bedroom, Jon heard Zane's breath whistle through his teeth. "That's a significant amount of blood. There's not a body in here anywhere?"

They stood back, so the forensic team could access the bed without them being in the way.

"No, no body. Just a note saying 'Stay out of this,'" Jon said.

"With all that blood? Has to be a body somewhere."

Jon nodded. "Yeah, my thoughts, also. And that our rapist has escalated to the next step."

"If that's true, it wasn't here that the killing took place," the tech said. "Except for the one handprint, this blood is undisturbed. There's no way a body could've been here and then moved and it look like this. This blood was *poured* here."

Zane glanced over at him, tilting his hat back slightly with his finger. "So it's possible that we don't have a dead body somewhere?"

The tech looked up. "It's possible this isn't even human blood. I think it is, but we'll know for sure pretty quickly once we get back to the lab. The way it was poured, it came in some type of container. So there may not be a dead body, just a wasted donation."

"I hate that this happened," Zane said as they watched the techs continue to work. "But it may be a break for us."

"I agree," Jon said. "And beyond that, there are only so many people who know Sherry has been working with us. Almost all of them are in law enforcement."

It was the reason Jon had *two* people out watching Sherry at the car. As of right now, he didn't trust anybody, especially not with her life.

It was possible that word had leaked out that Sherry was helping them; they hadn't been keeping it a secret. The mayor's office knew, everyone at the department knew, the victims and their families had been contacted, so they knew. Mayor Birchwood might even have included the info in his statement, although not mentioning her by name.

Whoever did this could've heard about Sherry from someone else; then finding her house wouldn't have been that hard.

Jon's gut was telling him it was someone with firsthand information who had done this.

If so, this case had just taken a whole new step into more complicated.

Chapter Eighteen

Jon observed the forensic team for a while longer and then left it in Zane's hands. There was nothing more he could do there and he needed to get Sherry to a safe place.

He was relieved to find her still sitting inside his car with the two patrol officers right where he'd asked them to stay. He released them to other duties and got in next to Sherry.

"Hey, how are you hanging in there?" He kept his tone as soft and even as possible.

She was staring down at the bottle of water and crumpled paper towels in her hand. "I couldn't get all the blood off," she whispered.

She turned her palm around to show him. Jon took her hand in his, which was icy to the touch, and stroked it softly. He knew partially congealed blood could be a beast to remove. "Let's get you to my place so you can take a shower. It will come off, I promise."

She just nodded, still looking down at her hand.

She didn't say anything the entire drive to his condo, which was relatively near the station. He didn't try to talk. What could he said anyway?

He didn't even want to think about what this blow to her psyche meant for the investigation overall. Looking over at her colorless face, he couldn't imagine asking her to just buck up and interview another woman tomorrow.

So although they had narrowed the suspect pool to someone who knew Sherry was working with them, they still didn't really have any suspects whatsoever. And had probably lost Sherry, the person who had been in the best position to help them.

He pulled the car into a spot in the underground parking of the condo unit and went around to help Sherry out. He wished he could've brought some of her clothes, but he knew they were all part of the crime-scene investigation at her house. Maybe tomorrow, if the scene was cleared, he could run by and grab her something. Tonight she'd just have to sleep in one of his shirts.

Once up the elevator and inside his unit on the sixth floor, he took her straight into the bathroom. No point in showing her around; the two-bedroom place wasn't very big, and she was in no shape to process anything.

She was still staring down at her red fingertips and palm. There really wasn't a lot of blood still on them, but the color was odd, as if she'd colored them with a red marker.

"Do you want to take a shower or a bath?"

She looked at him as if she didn't quite understand the question.

"How about a shower?" he continued. It would be better to let all the water ease down the drain.

He helped her out of her shoes and clothes, laying them over the edge of the tub, then turned the water on, almost as hot as he could stand.

Was it really only twelve hours ago when he and Sherry had been laughing in the shower together? Now he led her stiff body into the opening, lovemaking the furthest thing from his mind.

He stayed right there with her for those first few minutes, to make sure she was okay. Slowly he could see awareness come back into her eyes as she stood under the heated spray. She looked over at him.

"You okay?" he asked.

She nodded, then closed her eyes, turning and lifting her face to the spray.

Jon stepped back and closed the shower door. At least she was reacting, rather than standing there just looking so numb.

He went into the kitchen and heated up a can of soup and made some sandwiches. Neither of them had eaten, and although he didn't think she would feel like it, he still wanted to make sure she had the option.

He went into his bedroom and grabbed a T-shirt. It would be more than large enough for her to sleep in.

The shower was still running when he stepped back into the bathroom.

"You doing okay in there?" he asked. "Finally thawed out?"

When she didn't answer, he opened the shower stall door. "Sherry?"

She was scrubbing at her hand with the washcloth. He reached in to stop her, but she snatched her hands away, turning her back to him.

"Sherry, listen to me. The blood is gone, sweetie. I promise."

"My hand is still red."

"Your hand is red now from the hot water and from rubbing it so hard." He put both hands on her shoulders and turned her around gently. "There's no more blood."

He was getting wet from the shower spray ricocheting off her and the walls, but he didn't care. He reached down and took the washcloth from her. This time she didn't fight him.

"Let's get you out of there." He turned off the water and guided her from the shower. He wrapped her in a towel.

"You got wet, too," she whispered then touched him on the chest where he was most wet.

"That's okay. It's basically how I do laundry anyway."

A ghost of a smile. That was good. At least she was now focused on what was going on rather than nonexistent blood on her fingers. He gave her his shirt and helped her slip it over her head.

"How about if you get a little something to eat? Then we can see how you're feeling."

"I don't know if I can eat much, but I'll try."

She managed to get down half a sandwich and half of the glass of wine he put in front of her. He finished everything she didn't eat.

She had one leg bent and her knee propped up under his T-shirt, sitting across from him at the small kitchen table. She wrapped her arms around her knee and laid her head down.

"Do you want to watch some TV?" he asked. "Get on the computer?"

He hoped she wouldn't want to do either, because news of the break-in at her house might already be leaking onto the local news. Not to mention the mayor had given his update around 7:00 p.m., which was sure to be repeating now on the 10:00 p.m. news. Jon would like to know how the mayor did, but that could wait until tomorrow.

"No, not really. I think I just want to go to sleep, if that's okay?"

He reached out and tucked a strand of her hair behind her ear from where her head was resting on her knee. "That's more than okay. It's probably the best thing for you right now."

She nodded and he helped her up, slowing as he led her out of the kitchen. Should he put her in his bed? He wasn't even sure if she would want him in the bed with her. She might just want and need her space.

He would put her there anyway. If she said anything, he would understand and would sleep on the sofa bed in the second bedroom.

"Is this okay?" he asked as he led her to the king-size bed in the middle of the room.

She turned from the bed to look at him. "Is this where you'll be sleeping, too?"

"If that's all right with you?"

"Yes. I don't want to be anywhere by myself tonight."

He wrapped his arms around her and pulled her in to his chest. "You definitely don't need to be alone tonight or any time in the foreseeable future, until you feel like you're ready."

"Thank you for helping me," she whispered into his chest. "I'm sorry I never seem able to handle anything."

"Hey, what happened at your house would spook anyone, even more so someone like you who's already suffering from post-traumatic stress. So no more nonsense about not being able to handle anything."

She smiled, but she didn't believe him, he knew. He helped her get into bed and climbed in next to her, pulling her close.

"I know you probably have things to do. I'm okay."

He needed to make a couple of phone calls, check the progress of the crime-scene investigation and report what had happened to Omega Sector. And he would, in just a minute.

Right now he held her against him.

It didn't take long, much shorter than he would've thought, for her to fall asleep. He shouldn't have been surprised. She had been up most of the night last night, but for very different reasons. She was exhausted, physically and emotionally.

He eased her from beside him and stretched her on a pillow, then walked around the bed and covered her with the comforter. She never even stirred.

In the kitchen he made the call to Zane Wales first.

"Hey, Hatton. Is Sherry doing okay?" Zane asked after the first ring.

"Yeah, she's sleeping. How did it go at her house?"

"Pretty routine. Lab took everything they needed, including her entire mattress."

That was fine, she would never have been able to get the blood out of that anyway. He couldn't even imagine the emotional chaos that would cause her, given how long she had scrubbed her hand.

"Did they find anything of interest anywhere else in her house?"

"No, it looks like all the attention was concentrated on the bed. Symbolism, I guess. They're running any prints they can find in the house, especially in the master bed and bath. They eliminated Sherry's, of course."

Jon rubbed his forehead. "Mine are going to be there, too. We should probably prepare the lab for that."

"Did you touch something when you initially went into the room?"

Jon could hear the surprise in the younger man's voice. Rightfully so. Disturbing a crime scene when there was no imminent danger would be a pretty rookie move. "No."

"Then why would your prints be—? Oh."

Jon could almost hear the pieces clicking into place for Wales.

"Is there any particular place I should warn the lab about?"

"Living room. Bedroom. Bathroom." Jon was pretty sure he hadn't touched anything in the kitchen, but wasn't completely certain. "Hell, the whole damn house."

"Got it." The young detective was wise enough not to crack any jokes.

"What did they find out about the blood?"

"Definitely human. Good news and bad news there," Zane said. "Good news is a local blood bank truck was broken into sometime today. A few pints of blood were taken. They didn't even notice it was missing until this afternoon."

"So hopefully there's no dead body waiting around for us to find."

"That's what I was thinking. It would certainly be easier to pour blood from donated bags than to collect it from a victim into something and then pour it on the bed."

"All right, thanks for keeping me posted. When do you think they'll clear Sherry's house? I'm not letting her out of my sight until we catch this guy, but she could use some of her stuff."

"I'm sure we can probably get in there tomorrow."

She'd just have to stay in his T-shirt until then, which didn't bother Jon a bit, although he wished it was under different circumstances. He said goodbye to Zane, promising to check in tomorrow, although explaining he would not be there in the morning. Making sure Sherry was all right was his top priority. Then he placed a call to Omega.

It was nearly ten in the evening, so the call

was forwarded from the office to Steve Drackett's cell phone.

"I saw the Corpus Christi mayor on the news tonight. He did great. You must have done some coaching with him," Steve said by way of greeting.

"I did. He's pretty levelheaded, willing to listen. Wants to keep the city from becoming any more panicked than it already is."

"What did you think of his speech?"

"I haven't seen it yet."

"Really?"

"We had a situation here, Steve." Jon explained what had happened at Sherry's house. "Looks like the blood may have been stolen from a local blood bank and isn't from an actual body. So that's a relief at least."

Steve finished Jon's thought for him. "But Sherry is a target."

"Well, I don't plan to let her out of my sight, so he'll have to come through me if he's going to get to her."

"It also sounds like this guy is a little nervous about her involvement," Steve said.

"After seeing her work today, he ought to be. I still don't think any of the victims saw his face, but the way Sherry is able to walk them through the events? She's good, Steve."

"Maybe I need to look into bringing her on full-time at Omega."

That appealed to Jon on so many different levels it scared him. So he just grunted in noncommittal agreement.

He heard a noise from the bedroom. "I've got to go. I'll update you tomorrow if anything new happens."

"Okay. Be careful, Jon. Don't stretch yourself too thin. That's how mistakes happen."

Jon said goodbye, turned out all the lights and double-checked the locks on the front door. He looked in on Sherry, who was shifting restlessly but was still asleep.

After a quick shower, he slipped into a pair of gym shorts. He normally wouldn't wear anything to bed, but he didn't want to panic Sherry in any way if she woke in the middle of the night. Didn't want to trigger anything that might scare her more.

He got into bed and pulled her next to him, relieved when she sank closer to him rather than pulling away. He tucked her to his side and wrapped his fingers in her hair close to her scalp, kissing her forehead. He would do whatever he had to, to keep her safe.

He thought about what Steve had said about wearing himself too thin and making mistakes.

When it came to Sherry's safety, mistakes were not an option.

Chapter Nineteen

Sherry's eyes popped open and she struggled to remember where she was. The predawn light allowed for just enough visibility to see that she wasn't in her own bed. And then it all came rushing back to her.

Her house. The blood.

At least for the second morning in a row, Sherry wasn't cold. She knew that was because of the big heater of a man sleeping next to her, arms keeping her tightly held to him even in his sleep. She wanted to ease away from him, make sure she didn't wake him. But she wanted his warmth more, so she stayed where she was.

She was never going to forget the sight of all that blood. She had to fight the urge to try to rub it off her fingers again, although she knew there wasn't any there. It was difficult to keep the panic at bay.

The rapist had been in her house.

Yesterday Jon had asked if she'd wanted to

go home while he met with the mayor. What if she had done that? Would she have walked in to find the rapist in her house? Had he sat there watching her house, waiting to see if she would come home?

Would she have opened her door to his knock and been attacked by him, too, like Tina and Jasmine and the other women?

Would that have been *her* blood on the bed?

Even Jon's warmth wasn't enough to keep out the chill that ran through her system at that thought.

She couldn't stay in the bed any longer. She tried to ease out without waking him, but she'd just barely swung her legs over the side of the bed when his arm reached over and touched her on her hip.

"Hey." His voice was husky with sleep. "You doing okay?"

"Yeah." She glanced at him over her shoulder. He looked tousled but strong and capable. She wanted to ease back onto the bed, into his strength. "I'm not going to freak out or anything. I was just going to take a shower. I'm sorry I woke you. Go back to sleep."

His hand tightened on her hip, pulling her back toward him.

There was nothing she wanted more than to do that. To bask in his warmth, to lean on his strength.

She was ashamed of how she'd reacted last

night. Surely Jon hadn't signed on for mass hysterics when he'd spent one night with her. She hardly wanted to be around herself this morning. She couldn't imagine he really wanted to be, either.

He was a good guy. The type that wouldn't turn away from a damsel in distress, so to speak, no matter how much he wished she would pull it together.

So she wasn't going to let herself lie back down and draw from his strength. She needed to find her own strength.

She slid so she was just beyond his reach and she could face him. His eyes narrowed as he withdrew his hand, but she ignored that. One thing had really weighed heavily on her mind, something she had to know right away.

"Did they find the person that blood belonged to? There wasn't a dead body at my house, was there?" The thought that she might have tripped over a dead body did not help with the staying-calm-and-strong plan.

"No, as a matter of fact the forensic lab doesn't think the blood was from anybody being harmed. A blood bank truck was broken into yesterday. Donated blood was stolen."

"So no one was hurt?"

"We don't know definitely, but we are working based on that assumption as of right now."

"Thank God." She felt as if a weight had been

lifted from her chest. The thought that the maniac had killed someone to get her attention had been even more traumatic. The blood had been bad enough.

"Yes, it was definitely good news."

He looked so appealing lying there, arms tucked under his head against the pillow. The bed sheet had fallen low on his hips, revealing his chest and abs. She knew he was wearing shorts, but she also knew it wouldn't take much to have those off him.

The desire to crawl to him and kiss her way down that chest and abs—and beyond—was almost overwhelming. But after last night she wasn't even sure that was what he wanted anymore and could admit to herself that she was too cowardly to try to study his face for fear of what she might find there.

Not coldness—she knew he wouldn't be cold or unkind. It wasn't in his nature. No, she was afraid that if she looked in his eyes she would find *warmth* where yesterday there had been *heat*.

That he would gladly be her friend but had enough sense to realize he didn't really want the emotional messiness that would come along with continuing to be romantically involved with her.

She remembered him having to get soaking wet in the shower last night to get her to stop scrubbing her hand. So, yeah, she wouldn't blame him for deciding to firmly park in the friend zone. As much as she'd wanted to make her way over to his mostly naked body with her mostly naked body, she was afraid if she did he might gently stop her.

Then an even more horrifying thought: maybe he *wouldn't* stop her. Just let things continue out of kindness. Pity.

She couldn't stand the possible thought. She slid a little farther away without making eye contact.

"Yeah, I'm just going to take a shower, okay?" She smiled as best she could before walking away.

SEEING SHERRY'S FACE as she had walked out of her house last night after she'd witnessed the crime scene had been disturbing. It was an image burned into his mind that he wasn't likely to forget for a long time.

But, honestly, that tiny fake smile she'd just given him before heading toward the shower was every bit as disturbing.

Jon wasn't sure exactly what was going on, but he didn't like it. He got up and wandered over to the window that looked out on the city as the sun began to rise and it began to wake up.

He didn't expect Sherry to jump into bed with him. Hell, after what had happened last night, if she decided she was sleeping on couches for the foreseeable future, he wouldn't be able to blame her. He definitely didn't expect her to feel all romantic after her house—and her emotions—had just been so brutally violated.

But whatever had just happened a couple of minutes ago? Whatever was going on in that head of hers? Jon really didn't like it.

He hadn't wanted to make any sexual advances because it seemed in bad taste after what she'd been through. Yet Jon felt he had made a critical tactical error by letting her get up from the bed and go into that shower alone.

The biggest part of him—and other *specific* parts of him—all but demanded he rectify that error by following her in there and making love to her until neither of them was thinking about anything from yesterday.

Mentally he knew he should give her some space. She'd been through another trauma after weeks of already balancing in a delicate emotional state. Yeah, she'd had a little bit of a rough time last night, but the fact that she was coherent and functioning this morning just showed her considerable mental and emotional strength.

The scene of her scrubbing her hand in the shower had been scary, and for a few minutes Jon had thought he was going to have to call in professional help. A doctor-prescribed sedative would not be unheard of in this situation, maybe even advisable.

She had pulled it together, though, had even managed to eat a little bit before going to sleep. She'd had a few bad dreams during the night, he'd been able to tell—whether they were specifically about her house or not he didn't know—but she hadn't woken up sobbing or screaming.

Again, given that her mind was already dealing with the trauma of her work from the past few months, and that she'd been dealing with that *alone* without any sort of support system…last night could've—probably *should've*—emotionally crippled her. But it hadn't.

All in all, she was doing pretty damn good in Jon's opinion.

So what was it that was bothering him so much about their little talk a few minutes ago?

He'd seen her glance over at him, had thought she might instigate something physical as they both sat on the bed. He'd sat back against the pillows in the most casual pose he could muster, wanting her to know she was welcome to ease on over but that it definitely wasn't expected.

He'd been sure she was about to ease. His body tightened now with him just thinking about it.

But then she'd stopped. Shut down. Refused to look him in the eye. Given him that disturbing little smile that didn't come anywhere close to her gorgeous blue eyes, and had all but run for the shower.

Suddenly Jon understood why he was so disturbed with her behavior: she was shutting him out.

Jon turned from the window and walked to the closed bathroom door. Shutting him out was unacceptable. His hand was on the doorknob and he was turning it to open the door when he stopped.

Had she been shutting him out or had she just needed space?

He let go of the knob. If she needed time to mentally and emotionally regroup, he should give her that. But he sure as hell didn't want to.

He walked into the condo's little kitchen to make coffee and think about anything else except her in the shower. And what they had done in the shower yesterday morning. Because that was not going to result in him leaving her alone.

He took stock of what food was in the cabinets. He didn't have much to eat here. He preferred eating out to cooking. He didn't even have Sugar-O's, but he did have some bread to make toast—enough to get them through this morning. They would need to get some real groceries if they were going to be staying here a lot more.

Jon needed to figure out logistically how he was going to manage working on the case. Thinking the rapist might be someone connected to the police department totally put a new spin on things. He didn't want to take Sherry there, not that he expected her to be doing any work today anyway. And he definitely did not plan to leave her alone.

"Hey."

Jon turned as he heard her soft voice from the kitchen doorway. She still had his shirt on but also had put on her jeans from yesterday. She still wasn't quite looking him in the eye.

"Hey. Shower okay?" He kept his distance, leaning against the counter, not wanting to spook her in any way.

"I didn't nearly scrub my hand off, if that's what you mean." Her short laugh was completely devoid of humor.

She was embarrassed by how she'd reacted last night. Was that what this was all about? She was afraid he couldn't deal with the drama?

He all but rolled his eyes. She'd obviously never been around the Omega Sector office before. She had nothing on some of the stuff that happened around there.

Jon walked up to her and put his hands gently on her waist. He didn't want to come on too strong in case his assumptions were incorrect. But he definitely didn't want her standing there looking all uncomfortable, thinking he didn't want her.

Because if she responded to him he wasn't sure they would even make it to the bedroom.

He might have to lay her down right here on the kitchen table. And, honestly, he wasn't sure that table would support both of them.

He'd sure as hell like to find out, though.

"Sherry." He pulled her closer to him and hooked a finger under her chin, since she still wouldn't look him in the eyes. "If you need space, that's fine. But if for one second you think that—"

His sentence was cut off by a loud knocking on the door.

Jon released Sherry and ran in to grab his Glock on the bedside table. He pulled her inside the bedroom as the knock came again.

"Stay here."

"Why do you have your gun?" She was looking him in the eyes now, her own huge in her face.

"Because I haven't let anyone know where I'm staying. So nobody should be knocking on my door."

Chapter Twenty

She was seeing a whole different side of Jon. Hard. Physical. Dangerous. He tended to use his mind for every part of the job she'd seen so far. But right now Sherry had no doubt that Jon Hatton, gun in hand, was also a physical force to be reckoned with. Whoever was coming through that door was going to have to make it through Jon.

That was not going to be easy.

Sherry stayed in the bedroom doorway, which allowed her to see what was going on in the kitchen without being in Jon's way.

He stuck his eye up to the peephole then pulled it away quickly, obviously not wanting to make himself a target if someone was waiting with a gun on the other side.

Sherry watched as Jon shook his head and put his gun down on the table.

A knock on the door again. "Hatton, wake the hell up!" From the other side.

As he unlocked the chain on the door, he turned back to her. "I'm sorry for everything that's about to happen in the foreseeable future."

"What?" She took a step closer. "What do you mean?"

Jon opened the door and two men walked in.

"It's about damn time," one of them, the one with brown hair—just a touch too long to be conventional—and giant biceps said, looking at Jon as he strolled in. "I know you like to make sure your skin-care regimen is perfect in the morning, but seriously, leaving us out in the hallway like that?"

"Liam," Jon said in greeting, shaking his head. He shook the hand of the other man—handsome as sin, with some sort of Asian heritage—who walked in behind Liam. "Hi, Brandon. I guess Steve sent you guys."

"You know Drackett. Always afraid everyone is lonely," Liam drawled and then noticed Sherry. "I see that is not the case."

Liam, gorgeous and obviously well aware of that fact, walked over and wrapped his arms around Sherry. She let out a small squeak when he lifted her off her feet in a huge hug.

"Hey there, sweetheart. Why don't you and I sneak away right now, get married in Vegas, and I'll spend the rest of my life helping you forget the horrible time you ever spent with Jon Hatton?"

He kissed her straight on the mouth. She let out another squeak.

"Enough, Goetz," Jon said. "I'm sure Sherry would appreciate it if you would stop molesting her."

Liam winked at her but set her back down. "Some people don't know true love when it slaps them in the face, do they, sweetheart?"

Sherry giggled. It was truly the only option when faced with Liam's outrageousness, which was actually mostly for Jon's benefit, she was sure.

"Sherry, these are two of my colleagues from the Critical Response Division of Omega Sector, Liam Goetz and Brandon Han."

Liam winked at her again. "Introductions are obviously not necessary for me and my true love."

"It's nice to meet you, Sherry." Brandon offered his hand to her.

She shook his hand. "Sherry Mitchell."

Liam went over to pour himself a cup of coffee "Soon to be Mitchell-Goetz."

Jon came over and pulled a chair out for Sherry to sit at the table, then took the seat next to her. "Are you guys here for a reason besides for me to pound on Goetz when he continues to get out of line?"

Liam gave a dramatic wounded face from over at the coffeemaker.

"Actually, yes," Brandon said, pulling out a large stack of files. "Drackett said you mentioned that the police department may be compromised. So he sent us with a copy of all the case files, thinking maybe we can work here."

Brandon turned to Sherry. "Sorry about what happened at your house, by the way."

"Thanks." She turned and looked at Jon. "What do you think is wrong at the police department?"

Jon shrugged. "Zane and I both agreed that whoever did that to your house yesterday might have connections to the Corpus Christi PD."

"Because of the note saying 'Stay out of this'?" she asked.

Jon nodded. "Exactly. People with connections to the department had the most knowledge of you helping us in the case."

"But it wasn't exactly a secret. It could've been someone not directly related, who just heard about it," she murmured.

He took her hand. "Absolutely. I'd rather not take a chance having you at the precinct if we have other options. Like working here."

Sherry nodded. "Okay. We'll still need somewhere for me to interview the other victims."

"No one expects you to do that today. Least of all me." He gave her hand a squeeze. "It's okay to rest, take it easy."

Sherry didn't want to rest. Resting meant too

much time to think. To feel useless. To give the attacker more time to plan for his next victim.

"Han is a gifted profiler, one of the best Omega has," Jon continued. "Goetz is more muscle. Actually, I think he might currently be working as a janitor."

Liam shrugged. "Hey, we can't all sit around overthinking everything, like these two. I'm more of an action man myself. You ever get yourself in a hostage situation, trust me, you'll want me rather than Tweedledum and Tweedledee here. And, by the way, we janitors prefer the term 'custodial engineers.'"

Even Jon snickered at that one. He had introduced them as colleagues, but they were much more than that. They were his friends. People he trusted. Even despite the bickering, she could already see an ease in Jon that hadn't been there before.

"Actually, I'm staying to help," Brandon said. "Liam's just passing through on his way to another case."

"Of course, I'm going to try to talk Sherry into coming with me." Liam came over and stood behind her chair and began rubbing her shoulders. "We'll have much more fun than you'll have here with fuddy-duddy," he said in an exaggerated stage whisper.

"You know what?" Jon said, standing and rolling his eyes. "Why don't you go get some groceries while the adults do some work?"

"Only if Sherry comes with me," Liam said.

There was a moment of silence, of seriousness, between the two men. Something passing between them that she wasn't sure she totally understood but knew it was Jon passing her over to Liam.

"If you feel up to going with Liam, to getting some fresh air for a few minutes, that might be a good idea," Jon said to her. "I'd like to run a few aspects of the case by Brandon. Get his opinion as a profiler."

"Yeah, no problem," Sherry said with a chipperness she didn't feel. "Just let me grab my bag."

Sherry felt a weight in her chest and not because she was going to the grocery store. Jon was right, getting out of the condo would probably do her good. This just confirmed that she'd been right: Jon really had decided they were better off as friends.

If he was still interested in her, he wouldn't be sending her off with his handsome, charismatic friend who wanted to steal her away. She knew Liam was just joking in all his grandiose gestures, and she, of course, wasn't taking him seriously. But she knew if the roles were reversed and one of her friends was skirting around, making eyes toward Jon, there would be no way in hell she'd send them off alone for more flirty fun.

Jon obviously did not feel the same way.

"I HEAR AVOCADOS are an aphrodisiac food," Liam said, holding one up at the grocery store a little while later, waggling both eyebrows. "If not, you can still make some awesome guac with it. So a win either way."

Liam had been making similar outrageous comments throughout their entire time at the store. On any other day Sherry would've laughed and gotten into the whole act with him. But she just couldn't seem to work her way past the heaviness in her midsection at the thought that Jon didn't really want her anymore.

"Hey, blue eyes." Liam wrapped an arm around her. "What's going on inside that head of yours? You sad because of what happened in your house yesterday? That's messed up, by the way."

She shrugged as they walked down the grocery aisle. "Yeah, that was really bad. And I kind of freaked out last night." She explained about trying to scrub the nonexistent blood off her hands.

"Doesn't sound too unreasonable to me."

"It's not just that. I've also been having some post-traumatic-type symptoms the past couple of months. Cold spells. Not being able to draw."

Liam nodded. "Having negative emotional reactions—nightmares, insomnia, eating issues, substance abuse—are common problems among agents and officers their first couple of years. So don't feel like you're the only one. Eventually you learn to distance yourself a little from the emotional ugliness. Find some way to ground yourself."

"Yeah, Jon wanted to help with that, and probably could have. But my previous trauma symptoms coupled with last night's little interlude? I'm afraid it's kind of ruined everything between Jon and me. I think he wants to put a little distance between him and my crazy. For which I can't blame him."

"Did he actually say that to you?"

Sherry bit her lip. "Not in those exact words."

Liam rolled his eyes. "Did he say that to you in any words at all?"

"How could he not be thinking it, Liam? I'm one step away from being certifiably committed."

"Hatton? Please, girl. Hatton is the one that keeps us all together back at Omega. If he bailed every time someone went a little crazy, he'd spend his entire life running. Jon lives for the 'help me help you' stuff."

"Yeah, well, you guys are all friends. Jon and I are...well, let's just say we'd spent a grand total of one night together before the incident last night and me dumping my crazy on him. We'd only known each other a couple of days before that, so it's not like we have some friendship to ground us."

Liam stopped walking and smiled down at her. An authentic smile that had nothing to do with jokes. It changed the entire look of his face. "So Hatton finally jumped in headfirst with someone. About damn time. He usually overthinks a relationship to death before getting involved with anybody."

"Really?"

Liam nodded. "If he jumped in with you, it's because he wasn't thinking, he was *feeling*. That's important. I've known Jon a lot of years and have never known him not to overthink a relationship. To just *feel*."

Sherry wasn't convinced. "I saw the look between you before we left. The bro-code look that said, 'Hey, yeah, can you take her off my hands?'"

Liam laughed. "Well, you might need to brush up on your bro-code translating skills, because what that look actually said was, 'Hey, there's a maniac out there, so be damn sure you're watching over her because she's important.'"

Sherry didn't know if she could believe him or not. "Really?"

"Oh, sweetheart, as much as I'd like to steal you away, I could feel his eyes shooting daggers into the back of my skull the moment I touched you in the condo. I've kissed everyone he's ever known, including his mother, and he's never had any sort of reaction. This morning? He was ready to rip my head off."

"He didn't say or do anything."

"Trust me, I know. Han noticed, too, I'm sure. Although he's too polite to say anything about it. Trust me more about this—Jon Hatton can handle whatever 'crazy' you've got to throw at him, although I can tell by talking to you that your crazy is not nearly as toxic as you think it is."

"But—"

"When it comes to Hatton, there are no buts. Once he's decided you mean enough to him for him to help you shoulder your burden, it doesn't matter how big that burden is. He's going to help. He's decided that with you. And the amount of time spent together has nothing to do with the decision."

Could Liam be right?

"Oh, I am always right, darlin'." He answered her unspoken question as if he could read her mind. "Now let's get the groceries and get back so we can put your poor beau out of his misery."

Chapter Twenty-One

"I was looking at these files on the way down. This is a pretty interesting guy you've got here," Brandon said, reading back through the account of the third victim.

Jon knew for Brandon Han to say someone was "interesting" meant they had an unusual perpetrator on their hands. Brandon was a certified genius. He had something like three advanced degrees, could speak a dozen different languages and could run multiple different scenarios in his head at the same time like a computer.

The man was nicknamed "The Machine" because of that, although Jon didn't think people called him that to his face.

When Brandon began really looking at all the angles of a crime, it was a sight to behold—almost spooky. And for him to call someone "interesting" meant the rapist probably had a genius IQ, which wasn't surprising given the complete lack of evidence at the crime scenes.

"There doesn't seem to be any rhyme or reason to how he picks his victims," Jon said in agreement. "The women are different ages, different heights, weights, body sizes, have different hair color, hell, even skin color as of the last victim. None of them knew each other and all are from different socioeconomic backgrounds. Some well-off, some barely making by. One was a student."

"That's what I mean. Interesting. Serial rapists almost always tend to have a type. A pattern or ritual they are following."

"Yeah, well, if he does, I can't see it. I've tried to back away from it, to see if I can spot the pattern if I look at it from a further distance, but, honestly, I've got nothing."

"Maybe it's not the women who are his MO. Maybe it's the situation itself."

Jon nodded. "I thought that, too. There are really only two similarities in all the cases. They all occurred in doorways and they all involved the perp striking the women immediately to stun and effectually blind them, but not hard enough to do permanent damage."

Brandon lined up the hospital photos of all six women next to each other. Their bruised faces placed so closely together were a gruesome sight. "The attacks all happened at different times of day, different days of the week, right?"

"Yes. A week to two weeks between each attack—but no set length of time in between." That had been one of the first patterns Jon looked for. "Most at the women's homes, although one was at a hotel."

"The locations themselves could be an important role," Brandon said. "Especially once the city became aware there was a serial rapist at large. He had to choose places where he wouldn't be noticed or identified."

"Yes, so that has to take some planning."

"Absolutely."

"And the bruising." Brandon pointed to the pictures on the table. "Looking at the women, it's easy to see that this is the same guy. You've got similar bruises in the same location of the face."

Jon agreed. "Guy is controlled. He's not hitting these women out of anger. He has a definite purpose in how he strikes them—it's part of his plan, of what he's trying to accomplish."

They both studied the pictures for a long time, thinking.

Jon leaned back in the kitchen chair, rubbing a weary hand over his face. "Brandon, tell me what I'm missing. You don't have to sugarcoat it or ease me into it to save my feelings. If you see something I've missed, just throw it out there."

"I know you do a lot more than profile and your job here—as it is everywhere—has been multifaceted and complicated." Brandon slapped him on his back. "That's why they sent you instead of me. To deal with all the other stuff I'm terrible at."

Jon rolled his eyes. "Hasn't that been a joy?"

"I wish I could just point out something obvious here that you've missed and say 'nanny-nanny-boo-boo, moron, now go arrest the bad guy.'"

Jon chuckled. "But you don't have anything obvious to point out."

"All I can give you is my opinion, which is no more or no less valuable than yours."

"I'll take it."

"This guy is all about the planning. I think the rapes themselves are almost secondary. The thrill for him is figuring out the who, when and where he's going to do it without getting caught."

Jon nodded. That made sense.

"This is very much about not getting caught. That's why he got so angry about you guys using Sherry. He's afraid she'll be able to help the victims remember something about him. I also think he feels like it's cheating of some sort on your part to bring her in at this stage of the game."

Could that be possible? It made sense in a twisted way.

"You're dealing with a bored genius. He knows how law enforcement works. He knows how forensics works. He knows how the human body works."

"Why do you say that about the body?"

"Like you said, he hits the women just enough to suit his purposes—making it so they're dazed and can't see him. That sort of control? You'd have to know a lot about your own strength and how the bones of the face are made up. None of those women have broken noses or cheekbones. That's deliberate."

"I definitely agree."

"Even more than that, I think it has to do with bruising on his hand. If he hit them hard enough to fracture cheekbones, it would leave marking on his hands for days that would be impossible to miss."

"That would explain why there are different amounts of time between each attack." Jon had to admit that made sense.

Brandon shrugged. "Don't know for sure, but waiting for his hand to completely heal would be a logical reason."

They studied the pictures.

"He wants a challenge," Brandon continued. "He's probably highly successful in whatever line of work he's in, which would definitely be white collar."

"Victim six, Jasmine Houze, thinks he was wearing a white office shirt. So literally white collar."

"I wouldn't be surprised if this guy is a CEO or something. He's used to planning things to the minutest detail, a habit that translates into his crimes. The rapes are his newest challenge, since he's probably bored in whatever field he works in. Although highly successful."

Brandon sat back, crossing his arms over his chest. "I think you're dealing with a bored genius who wondered for years what crimes he could get away with and then finally started putting them into practice."

Jon got the distinct feeling that concept might have struck just a little too close to home for Brandon. The man was a loner. Jon couldn't recall ever seeing him casually hanging out with anyone.

Not that he was a rapist or about to commit any other crimes. But the bored genius part? That was definitely Brandon.

"Jon, I wouldn't be surprised if he escalates. To use poker terms, you anted up, and he's calling. You brought Sherry into this, so he'll do something to counter."

"Speaking of Sherry, where the hell are they? It's not like we need groceries for a month."

"You worried about her safety or you worried about her with Liam?" Brandon asked.

"Safety, of course. Goetz is a putz."

A putz that women went gaga over. If he kissed Sherry again, Jon would have to see how good *his* knowledge of the human body was, because he'd definitely be trying to break Liam's nose.

"Maybe I should call them and make sure they're all right."

"If you're truly worried about safety, you know no one is going to get the drop on Liam. But if you're worried that he might be talking her into running away with him to a tropical island…" Brandon chuckled.

Liam was his friend, and Jon knew he didn't have to worry about him really trying to steal Sherry away. But all Jon could see was that pitiful smile she'd given him as she'd eased out of bed this morning, the one that had suggested she thought he didn't really want her.

He reached for his phone. He'd be damned if she'd turn to Goetz—who Jon was sure would be more than willing to comfort her—because she thought Jon didn't want her.

They needed to get back to the damn house. Right damn now.

He was looking up Liam's contact info when the door opened.

"Kids, we're home."

Liam was carrying two large bags of groceries. Sherry followed behind him, looking at Liam with that bemused, utterly charmed smile women tended to have around him.

Jon didn't think about what he was doing, he just grabbed Sherry and pulled her to him, kissing her soundly. He heard her startled gasp before she melted against him and wound her arms around his neck.

He didn't care about the other two men in the room, didn't care that they were sure to give him a hard time about this. All he cared about was making sure Sherry knew that *hell, yes* he still wanted her.

"Ahem, excuse me, I'm going to have to ask you to get your hands off my woman." Liam's words eventually penetrated Jon's mind and he stopped kissing her, reluctantly, although he kept her pinned to his side.

Liam wasn't actually even paying them any attention since he was putting groceries away. Brandon was studying the case pictures again.

Jon smiled down at Sherry. "I'm glad you two made it back okay and that this clown didn't talk you into eloping."

Liam sighed dramatically from across the room.

"Well, here was where I wanted to be." She smiled up at him, stealing his breath.

He trailed a finger down her cheek. "Here is where you're wanted."

"I'm sorry about freaking out last night."

"No apology necessary. You never have to be sorry for choosing to survive something. You said that to Jasmine, and it's just as true for you. Anytime I can help you do that, carry some of that burden for you, I'm glad to do so."

Sherry looked over at Liam, and Jon looked up in time to see him wink at her from where he was opening a box of cereal. Evidently the two of them had discussed Jon and freak-outs while they were away.

She eased away from him and walked over to the table, looking down at the pictures.

"Here, let me put those away," Jon said. "There's no need to look at them."

"No, it's okay." She put out an arm to stop him. "I'm done letting fear get the better of me. There's work to be done."

"Do you see, Jon?" Liam said as he shoveled a spoonful of cereal into his mouth. "Do you see why I'm so in love with her?"

Jon could definitely see why *he* was falling in love with her. Liam be damned.

"Sherry, it says here you project that the rapist is probably around five foot nine or ten?" Brandon asked, seemingly oblivious to everything else being said in the kitchen.

"Yes." She nodded. "That's based on the neck angle of victim number one—Tina Wescott— when he first entered her doorway. Hopefully I'll be able to confirm that when I talk to the other women."

Brandon looked over at Jon. "The rapist being that height—pretty short for a man—would fit the profile we were discussing earlier."

Jon held out a chair for Sherry and then sat in

the one next to her. "He's probably tried to over-compensate for his height his whole life. It may be why he chose rapes as his crime—because he's always felt like he had something to prove with women."

"Exactly," Brandon agreed. "The tattoo is interesting. It's placed on his body somewhere where you only see it if he decides to show it to you."

"I wouldn't be surprised if he has others," Jon said.

Brandon nodded. "Me, either. Honestly, I wouldn't be surprised to find he has tattoos commemorating his victims."

"I'll send locals out to tattoo shops to see if there are any repeat customers coinciding with the attack dates." It was a long shot, Jon knew, but was at least something. Although a man that smart probably wouldn't use the same shop more than once.

"I want to talk to the other victims," Sherry said. "We can't wait any longer. You'll just have to help me get through it."

Jon stretched his arm around the back of her chair and squeezed her. "Okay. I'll set them up. But I don't want to do it at the police station. I still am not sure one of those guys isn't the attacker."

Brandon shrugged. "Any number of law-enforcement officers—especially high-ranking or ones on the force for a long time—could fit the profile. They'd know how to hit. They'd know what to look for in a location where they wouldn't be seen. They'd know about forensic evidence and how not to leave any."

That was what Jon was afraid of. And he definitely wasn't going to keep working in their building if he was basically hand-delivering all the information the perp needed to keep successfully committing crimes.

"I'll go to their houses or wherever they're staying. That's probably better for them anyway," Sherry said.

"Are you sure?" he asked her. Yeah, things were becoming more critical. But Jon didn't want to lose sight of the fact that Sherry was still in a delicate emotional place. He wanted her help with this case, but he also wanted to make sure she was going to be able to function after it was over.

"I can do this." Her voice was stronger, more assured, than it had ever been when she was talking about the case. "Just don't let me go under."

"I won't." He kissed the side of her head as he stood to go make the calls.

He wondered if this bastard knew that by bringing the fight directly to Sherry's doorstep he would awaken the warrior in her rather than cause her to cower. It had been the wrong move on his part on multiple different levels.

And it was going to be the reason why they caught him.

Chapter Twenty-Two

True to her word, Sherry spent the next two days interviewing the other women. She worked with them tirelessly. She laughed with them, cried with them. She knew the most intimate details about their lives by the time she finished.

She was obviously much more comfortable—or at the very least much more focused—than she had been when interviewing Tina Wescott at the station a couple of days ago. Although there hadn't been any facial descriptions to draw, Sherry had been ready with her sketch pad. She'd been ready to work through any of her emotional walls and draw, if they did think of something.

For each interview she sat the woman facing a blank wall. And, as with Tina, walked them back to an hour before the crime. She would start by asking them for general descriptions, and then rewind and start again, each time focusing on different sets of details.

She was able to confirm that the man's

height was no more than five foot ten. More than one victim felt that he had darker skin. Not African-American, but highly tanned Caucasian or perhaps even of Mexican or South American descent. One woman remembered his shoes with vivid clarity.

Unfortunately, Nike sold a few hundred thousand pairs of those types of athletic shoes any given year.

Jon and Brandon had been with Sherry for each interview, although usually out of the way. Liam had left yesterday for his other case.

"She's really very good at what she does," Brandon observed.

"I know."

"She doesn't hold back, she gets right there into the moment with them. It's one of the reasons she's so good."

"It's also one of the reasons why she's suffering from post-traumatic stress," Jon said.

"Yeah, she'll have to find a way to protect herself better emotionally."

Jon had made sure he was always nearby in case the debilitating chills came back. A couple of times she had stopped and taken a break from an interview and sought him out.

Usually after he'd pulled her close, or they'd taken a walk, or a few deep breaths, she'd been able to pull herself out of the dark place she'd been heading.

"She's learning that taking a break for her own sanity is just as okay as the victim needing a break," Jon said. "She had the drawing skills and she had the obvious interviewing and people skills, so the Bureau scooped her right up."

"But nobody made sure she had the emotional resources to cope with what she was doing."

"Exactly."

"She'll get there."

"I plan to make sure of that." The more Jon knew her, the more he hoped being around to help keep her grounded would become a permanent job for him.

"Have you heard anything that seems to conflict with our profile?" he asked Brandon as Sherry finished talking to victim number four and was now making small talk.

"No, nothing."

"Anybody at the precinct fit the role?"

Brandon had been spending his spare hours at the Corpus Christi Police Department under the pretense of looking over the full case files, but really to get a read on possible suspects there.

"Only a couple."

"There are enough people there who seem to have impeded forward progress on this case to make me suspect them."

Brandon nodded. "Fortunately for them, being a jerk isn't a crime, otherwise we'd definitely be arresting some people."

"I was thinking that if someone knew we were looking for that particular tattoo he might try to cover it up, either with makeup or a shirt."

"Yeah, we can't legally ask everyone to show us their arms. Might make this investigation a whole lot easier if we could," Brandon said.

Jon's phone buzzed in his pocket. It was a text from Zane. Jon read it, then rubbed a weary hand across his face. "That was Wales. We've got another victim at Memorial."

They had all known it was coming, but had hoped they'd be able to get far enough ahead of the guy to stop him.

Brandon muttered an expletive.

"My feelings exactly," Jon said. "I've got to tell Sherry."

NOTHING SHE'D BEEN able to do had been enough. It was the thought that kept running through her head as she sat in the backseat of the car that raced toward the hospital.

"You don't have to go if you don't want to," Jon said, making eye contact with her from the rearview mirror. "I'm sure Brandon will take you to my place."

"I will," Brandon said. "Truly, Sherry. If you feel like this is too much for you, Jon and I would be the first to support you on that."

Sherry thought about it for a moment but knew she could do this. The past couple of days had been tough, but she had handled it. Hearing what these women had gone through—over and over—had threatened to trigger the debilitating chills, but when it had gotten to its worst, Sherry just called for a break.

Actually the first few times, Jon had seen what was happening and *he* had called for a break. But then Sherry recognized the pattern herself and had started doing it. For two years she'd been interviewing victims, careful to watch for when they needed a break and when they needed to stop altogether. Because at some point more harm than good could be done by continuing to push.

Why she never realized the same was true for herself was beyond her. As a forensic artist, Sherry was not only responsible for the mental and emotional well-being of the people with whom she spoke, but was responsible for that in herself.

She felt as though a choir of angels should be singing or something at her grand epiphany.

She knew it would change everything in her career. She looked down at the sketch pad in her hand. It was now full of drawings she'd made of the past two days. Nothing important to the case, but it at least meant her mind was freeing itself to draw again.

She trusted when the time came for her to draw a face for actual police work, she would be able to do it. That might be right now at the hospital.

So, no, she wasn't going to go home and hide and feel as if it was too much for her.

She reached up and touched Jon's shoulder. "Truly, I'm okay. I can do this, if I'm needed. If not, I'll just stay out of your way."

Jon reached up with his own hand and squeezed hers, then put it back on the wheel.

They pulled into the hospital lot and rushed into the trauma unit. Sherry silently hoped this would be the same as the last time they'd rushed here—a false alarm, so to speak, where the woman hadn't actually been raped.

But she knew when she saw the full magnitude of both the police and hospital staff fairly hovering in the hallway that they wouldn't be that lucky.

It was Zane who met them halfway in the hallway. For the first time Sherry had ever seen him, he had his cowboy hat in his hands rather than on his head. She was absently wondering why he would hide such a gorgeous head full of hair under that hat, and then she noticed his face.

Haggard. Stricken. Completely devoid of color.

This was a man hanging on by a thread.

"What, Wales? What is it?" Jon asked when Zane couldn't seem to get any words out. "Is it definitely the same guy? Same facial trauma?"

Jon looked toward the hospital room, highly focused on the case and not really noticing what was happening right in front of him.

"What, Zane?" Sherry reached out and touched him on his arm. "Was someone killed?"

Jon's attention refocused on the man in front of him. "Just say it."

"It's Caroline. Caroline is the victim."

Sherry took a step back, reeling into herself. No.

"Oh, my God." She felt Jon's arms come around her almost from a distance.

Bubbly, feisty, little Caroline? She couldn't be the victim of this monster.

"I—" Zane seemed lost. In shock. "I—"

Brandon made eye contact with Jon, then took over.

"Hey, man." Brandon put a guiding hand on Zane's back. "Why don't you come sit down over here?" He led Zane to some chairs, where he slid bonelessly into one, staring blankly ahead. Brandon sat with him.

"He's not okay," Sherry whispered.

"No, he's definitely not," Jon answered, his arm still around her. "None of us are okay, but Wales may never be okay again. I'm going to get someone to take you home."

"No!" Sherry leaned back from him. "She's my friend, Jon. I'm not going to go boo-hoo at your house while my friend is in there and needs support. My emotional state takes a backseat to what she needs right now."

Jon tugged her into his chest tightly. "Okay."

"I know you have stuff you need to do. I'm okay. Just get me in to see her as soon as you can."

"Are you sure?"

"More than positive. I'll sit with Zane while you and Brandon go work this situation." She looked at all the people milling around outside Caroline's door; they were almost like zombies. "Those people need somebody to lead them and tell them how they can best help."

She knew without a doubt Jon was the man for that job.

Jon turned to do his job, and Sherry walked over to the chair, relieving Brandon.

"Are you okay?" Brandon asked.

"Yes. I'm going to sit here with him. You go do your job."

Sherry wrapped an arm around Zane as she sat.

"Caroline is the strongest, most feisty gal I know," she said. "We will help her get through this."

"I should've been there," Zane said, sliding his hat in circles in his hands centimeter by centimeter. "I was supposed to have been there."

"Zane—"

"Caroline isn't stupid. She wouldn't just open her door to anyone when there's a maniac out on the loose. I was supposed to go to her house this afternoon, but decided not to go. Decided she wasn't what I wanted. Again. Like the dumb ass that I am."

Sherry wasn't sure what could be said to comfort the man. "Zane, you can't blame—"

Zane turned and looked Sherry in the eye. "She opened that door this afternoon thinking it was me. I know that with every fiber of my being. But it wasn't me. It was a monster."

Sometimes there weren't any words that could be said. Nothing would fix this. She rubbed his arm. "I'm so sorry."

"I'll have to live with that every day for the rest of my life." He crushed his hat with his fingers. "She's in a coma, Sherry. The trauma was much worse than the previous victims. Dr. Rosemont isn't sure when she'll wake up. *If* she'll wake up."

Sherry could feel tears pouring down her cheeks. "She's strong, Zane. A fighter."

"I should've been there."

Chapter Twenty-Three

"Are you sure Sherry is going to be okay?" Brandon asked as he caught up to Jon walking down the hall. "Caroline is her friend, right?"

Jon glanced at Sherry over his shoulder where she sat with Zane. "That woman has shown a measure of grit in the past forty-eight hours that is truly remarkable." Jon had seen seasoned agents crumple under less pressure.

"No arguments from me."

"I'm beginning to think there isn't anything that Sherry can't handle. She might have to work her way through some bad points initially, but she gets herself there."

It was downright impressive.

He realized Brandon was staring at him. "What?"

"First Derek, now you."

Derek was a member of Omega's SWAT team who was currently on his honeymoon or he would probably be here right now helping with this case. "First Derek what?"

"Nothing." Brandon slapped him on the shoulder, smiling. "You'll figure it out. You're smart."

Jon shook his head, turning his focus to the case at hand. The hospital hallway was crowded, even more than it had been with Jasmine Houze a week ago. Jon knew why.

Caroline was one of their own. The desire to stop this bastard had just shot through the roof. It also made for a very explosive *Texan* crowd that would need to be handled appropriately.

First he needed all the details from Dr. Rosemont about Caroline's condition. She was still in there with Caroline, but Jon spotted Dr. Trumpold, Sherry's "handsome" doctor—although Jon decided not to hold that against him this time—and cornered him to ask some questions.

"Dr. Trumpold, I just arrived. Can you give me any sort of update?"

"Agent Hatton."

Jon was a little surprised the man knew his name. That meant there had been too damn many victims brought in.

"I haven't been in there, of course. Dr. Rosemont and I have agreed that it's best for all male personnel to stay out of any of the victims' rooms unless they've been given express permission."

The man shrugged, hands in his lab coat

pocket. It wasn't difficult to see he felt frustrated for being left out of the loop.

"But from what I understand, Ms. Gill is in a coma," the doctor continued. "Evidently the craniofacial trauma was much greater this time."

Jon looked over at Brandon. "He's really escalated, then. Sick bastard."

"If you'll excuse me, gentlemen, I have to attend to some other patients. Dr. Rosemont should be out shortly."

Jon and Brandon turned back toward the door.

"A coma," Jon muttered. "That's not good. Maybe she saw something and he's trying to keep her quiet."

"It's possible. But with this guy, I think he would've finished the job and killed her outright. Made sure there was no chance she could identify him."

Jon agreed. This guy wouldn't leave loose ends.

"I think this has to do with Caroline's connection with Sherry. Pointing out that he knows things about her—who she's friends with—and that he isn't afraid to punish her for her continuing to help the police."

Jon could feel rage flow through him. He was more determined than ever to keep Sherry out of this madman's hands.

"That anger you're feeling? Everybody in this hallway is feeling the same thing," Brandon said as they looked at the twenty or thirty people standing around. "I know you think someone in the department could be the rapist, and I'm not discrediting that possibility. But everyone here is furious for what has happened to one of their own. And they're feeding off one another."

Jon agreed. They needed encouragement and they needed to be dispersed. He wasn't sure they were going to listen to him. He was still the outsider.

But he had to try.

Jon got their attention. "People, I know Caroline Gill appreciates your show of support here, but we're going to need everyone to leave."

There were some loud murmurs of disagreement. The men and women were angry and Jon had just given them a target at which to direct their anger: him.

"Look, I know you all care about Caroline, have worked with her, are friends with her. But right now you are needed elsewhere, doing your jobs."

An angry voice from the crowd shouted, "That's easy for you to say, you don't really know Caroline at all."

Jon took in a deep breath. "I know I don't. Not nearly as well as you guys. This is what I do know—when word gets out there has been another attack, the city is going to be tempted to tip over into panic. Each one of you is needed to stop that from happening."

"Do you think you know our town better than us?" A different voice this time.

"No. I do know that we need to work with the evidence we have. We need to hit the tattoo parlors again for information about the one piece of visual evidence we have. We need to be hitting the streets, seeing if any contacts—old, new or otherwise—have heard or seen *anything* to do with the attack. Most of all, we need to be a visual presence in the city, helping people stay calm."

"Why should we listen to you? You don't really care about us."

He wasn't getting through to them, Jon could tell. They were too incensed.

"No."

Jon was surprised to hear a voice from behind him as he tried to figure out what he could further say.

It was Zane. Cowboy hat back on his head.

"That sort of talk needs to end right now," Zane told them, his tone brooking no refusal. "Agent Hatton—Jon—has worked tirelessly on this case and it's time we all start treating each other like we're on the same side.

"There's a real bad guy out there," the detective continued, his voice breaking just slightly at the words, "and it's not Jon, or any member of the feds. It's time we pull together and stop this bastard."

People were nodding, responding to Zane the way they couldn't to Jon.

"So go do like you've been directed." Another voice this time. Captain Harris. "Do what Agent Hatton told you to do. We solve this, stop this, as a team. The city needs to see you right now and know you're there, like Hatton said. He may not be from Texas, but he's close enough in my book."

The leadership from these two men made all the difference. The officers and hospital workers began to disperse, a few even coming to shake Jon's hand. He promised to keep everyone updated.

"Thank you," he said to Captain Harris and Zane.

"I'm done messing around," Harris said. "He attacked one of our own. He's going down."

"I couldn't agree more."

SHERRY SPENT THE next thirty-six hours next to Caroline's hospital bed. Most of that time Zane sat there with her—when he wasn't pacing up and down the hallway. Sherry had at least gotten a little bit of sleep on the couch in the room. Zane hadn't even considered it.

The doctors still had no definitive answer for

when Caroline might wake up. She did have brain activity. That was the most important thing.

Jon had been in and out, willing to leave Sherry at the hospital as long as she promised to stay put and not leave alone under any circumstances. She knew Jon had other things to do besides babysit her: the crime scene, not to mention advising the mayor on further media issues.

Especially now that everyone was willing to listen to him, thanks to Zane's and Captain Harris's words at the hospital.

Caroline's face was hard to look at, the trauma so much more extensive than the other victims. Her nose was broken, cheekbone shattered. She would need reconstructive surgery, but they wanted to wait until she was out of the coma first.

Dr. Rosemont said Caroline might be able to hear what was going on around her, so Sherry tried to talk to her as much as she could. She even read to her from the local gossip magazines. Her voice was starting to get hoarse.

She was pretty sure Zane sat there and whispered in Caroline's ear when Sherry was sleeping. He was determined to let her know she wasn't alone.

Sherry hadn't seen much of Brandon. Jon said he was wandering around the police station and the mayor's office, anywhere that might have known about the connection between Sherry and the department.

"What is he doing?" she asked.

"Looking at people's hands," Jon said with a shrug. "The damage to Caroline's face couldn't be done without there being some sort of telltale sign on the perp's hands and knuckles."

She and Jon were sitting in the hallway outside Caroline's door. His arm was around her and she had her head on his shoulder. It felt good to be like this; to be close to him. Plus, it allowed them to talk, since Zane had finally fallen asleep sitting in the chair, his head propped next to Caroline's arm on the bed. Sherry didn't want to wake him.

"He's a mess. He blames himself," Sherry said.

"Yeah, I know. He's going to have to work through this in his own way."

"It's not his fault."

"Yeah, but nobody in the world is going to be able to make him believe that except him. Or maybe Caroline. I doubt even her."

They sat in silence for a while, just holding on to each other. She knew Jon probably had other things he needed to do.

"Do you have to go?"

His arm tightened around her. "Eventually. But not right now. Right now I'm not going anywhere."

Sherry snuggled in deeper.

A few minutes later Dr. Rosemont and some of the other hospital staff came running down the hallway and into Caroline's room. Sherry and Jon both jumped up.

"What's going on?"

Zane came out of Caroline's hospital room. "She woke up."

"Is she okay? Is she talking?" Sherry asked.

Zane smiled for the first time since Sherry had arrived at the hospital. "She told me I needed to take a shower."

The man then covered his face and started crying.

Sherry rushed up to put her arms around him. "She's going to be okay, Zane. She's awake. She's going to be okay."

"I know. I'm all right." He pulled himself together, then gave an embarrassed look at Jon. "Sorry."

"No need to apologize to me," Jon said, slapping him on the back. "Tears aren't weakness in a situation like this."

Jon knew Zane couldn't handle any more kindness than that, Sherry realized. Jon's ability to *handle* people maybe wasn't such a bad thing, after all.

"Caroline wants to talk to you two. She says she saw the man who attacked her."

As soon as the doctor let them through, they were by Caroline's side.

"Hey, sweetie," Sherry said. "I'm so glad you're awake."

Caroline grimaced. "I'm not. It was much less painful when I was sleeping." Her words were mushy from the swelling.

"We're going to up your pain medication, Caroline," Dr. Rosemont said. "There's no need for you to fight the pain right now. There will be plenty of time for that."

"Not yet," Caroline said. She turned her face toward Sherry and Jon even though she probably couldn't see out of either eye very well. "I saw him."

"That's what Zane told us, honey. Do you remember anything?"

"As soon as the door burst open, I knew what was happening. I knew I only had a second to get a look. I could see his fist coming toward me."

Caroline's breathing became more labored.

Dr. Rosemont took a step closer. "Let's stop for right now, Caroline," she said. "You can tell us this later."

"No, now." Caroline was adamant.

"Sweetie, we can wait." Sherry leaned close and murmured, "It's okay."

"No, you have to stop him now." She took a breath. "I didn't see his face because of the sunlight, but I did see his hair."

"His hair?" Sherry asked. "Tell me." She wished she had her sketch pad, but she wasn't about to leave to get it. She felt Jon put something in her hands. A notebook and pen.

It wasn't a sketch pad, but it was enough. Thank God for that man and his ability to see everything that was going on.

"He had long blond hair," Caroline whispered.

Sherry glanced at Jon. He had the same confused look on his face.

Long blond hair was weird. Or at the very least highly distinguishing, given the man's dark skin.

"Caroline, I don't mean any offense by this, okay? But are you sure about the hair?" Sherry asked as gently as she could.

Caroline tried to nod but then groaned in pain. "I *know* I saw his long blond hair lying against the side of his cheek when he turned to the side. Straight. Long—shoulder length. Yellow blond."

"Okay." Sherry sketched out a picture, leaving the face blank but with straight hair flowing on the sides.

"I knew what was going to happen. And I knew I had to keep this clear in my mind. It was the only way I could fight." Caroline's voice was getting weaker.

The doctor gave Sherry and Jon a pointed look.

"You did great, Caroline," Jon reassured her. "We're going to go now and get this info out to every officer in the city. You've done your job. You rest now."

"Okay." Caroline's voice was tiny. Heartbreaking.

"I'm staying here with her," Zane told them as they walked out. "Do you think her intel is correct?"

Jon looked over at Sherry.

She shrugged. "Memory is fragile. Contaminated within seconds. But Caroline was aware of what was happening, and is trained to be aware of what is going on around her. If she says the man had blond hair, I believe her."

"I do, too," Jon agreed. "I'm going to have Sherry draw something up and, like I told Caroline, we're going to get it out to every damn officer in the city."

Chapter Twenty-Four

Things moved faster than Jon could've dreamed. Especially now that the Corpus Christi PD had decided they were all on the same team. When he and Sherry arrived at the precinct, someone had already gotten all the materials out and ready for Sherry to draw her sketch. Sherry just sat and began working.

She drew a composite sketch based on the details she had gathered from all the victims. She based the facial size on averages of men around five foot nine. Put in generic features based on his possible Latin American or Mexican heritage given the skin tones Jasmine Houze recognized. Then she added the long, straight blond hair.

She handed it to Jon, shrugging. "It's the best I can do with the info I have right now."

Jon looked at it. To be honest, he didn't really think it was going to help. The features were too generic and the hair was too specific.

But he was willing to try. So he showed it to

Captain Harris and they sent it out electronically to every officer in the city. They agreed to wait to see what happened before putting the drawing on the news, knowing that would probably trigger the man to change his appearance if he hadn't done so already.

Under other circumstances the sketch might not have helped at all, but the locals were determined to find justice for Caroline. They were beating the pavement looking for the guy, working extra hours without pay for her.

One uniformed officer—the man deserved a medal in Jon's opinion—had gotten the sketch to his cousin who owned a chain of barbershops, feeling that the first thing someone like that would do was try to get rid of the identifiable hair.

Two hours later they had a call. Someone matching the description had come in asking for a haircut.

And he had tattoos on his arm.

The barbers had been instructed to stall him for as long as possible without cutting his hair, but to begin to slowly cut it if it looked as though the guy would leave.

Jon and Brandon had provided backup for the uniformed officers who had gone in to make the arrest.

The suspect had been getting his hair washed

by the barber at the time. It went down as one of the most bizarre arrests that Jon had ever seen.

And just as Caroline had said, the man had long blond hair. He was around five-ten, a young, tanned punk who had dyed his hair blond to stand out; to be cool.

Well, his need for cool was going to cost him the rest of his life in prison.

He was confident, cocky. Playing off the whole thing as if he had no idea what they were arresting him for. Sending sly looks in Jon and Brandon's direction.

"He's younger than I would've thought," Brandon said.

"Yeah, maybe we were dealing with a young, bored genius rather than someone established in a career," Jon responded, watching the officers walk him out to the car in cuffs.

Brandon shrugged. "That still works with the profile, I guess."

The skull on his arm was what had convinced them both. It wasn't exactly what Jasmine Houze had described—there were diamonds drawn in the eye sockets rather than targets—but as Sherry had said, memories were fragile. Given the circumstances, Jasmine's memory was pretty damn close.

The smile the guy gave them was malicious to the core. Jon felt relieved to have him off the streets. He wanted to see if Captain Harris would let Jon talk to the guy; see what he could get out of him. The blond hair and tattoo were pretty damning, but a confession would be the best way to make sure he went to prison for a long time.

THEY'D GOTTEN HIM. The excitement around the station was palpable. Evidently the guy had been getting his hair washed at the time of the arrest, which made everyone snicker. It was important to look pretty on your way to jail.

Jon had texted Sherry that he wanted to interview the suspect himself, which didn't surprise her at all. And it was fine. Sherry wanted to let Caroline and Zane know the good news face-to-face.

Maybe now Zane would be able to start forgiving himself.

She knew processing and questioning the suspect would take a long time. She just jotted a note for Jon to let him know where she was going and left it at his desk rather than disturb him with a text. She ended it with "You, me, celebration tonight. Naked. So tell Brandon to make other plans."

She folded it and wrote his name on the outside. Somebody might read it, but Sherry no longer cared if anyone knew about her and Jon.

Of course, he would be heading back to Colorado soon, now that the case was finished. Sherry wasn't going to think about that right now. Right now she wanted to share the good news about the arrest with her friends.

Caroline was sleeping, but they woke her to tell her. She tried to stay awake to talk to them about it but couldn't manage.

"She has a long path to recovery," Sherry told Zane.

Zane nodded. "Yeah, but catching that bastard was a big step."

"Let's just hope he confesses. That would make everything easier when they go to prosecute."

They talked for a few more minutes before Sherry stood to get back to the station.

Zane stopped her. "Sherry, do you mind going by Caroline's house and picking up a few things for her? You know, stuff that might make her feel more comfortable here? A gown and whatnot. I don't want to leave her."

She touched Zane's arm. "Sure. That's a really great idea. I'll just need to borrow your car."

"No problem. And her house is still a crime scene, so don't go near the front door area." Sherry could tell he had difficulty just forming the words.

Zane dragged some keys out of his pocket. "Here're the keys to my SUV and Caroline's back door. If there's a uniformed officer there, just have him call me for clearance."

Sherry drove to Caroline's house and got inside, avoiding the front hallway area altogether. She got the items she thought her friend would want—some pajamas and other clothes, her own pillow, the book on the bedside table—and put them inside Zane's SUV.

The big yellow Do Not Cross tape at Caroline's front door was difficult to look at. Sherry wondered if Caroline would ever be able to live here again.

Sherry decided it was time for her to face her own crime scene of a house. Although Jon had gotten her some of her own clothes, she hadn't been back there yet herself.

It was time to face that so she could move on. Better to do it now without an audience, even though she knew Jon would gladly have come with her. If she was going to have a breakdown again, she wanted to do it on her own.

She decided to walk. Her house was only a few blocks away if she walked along the shoreline. She took off her shoes and rolled up her jeans.

Sherry breathed in the heavy air of the storm that would be rolling in the next couple of hours. The waves were crashing higher and the beach was empty of almost everyone. Just how Sherry liked it. She smiled at a couple she passed as they strolled hand in hand, enjoying the roughness of the weather just as she was.

Now that the case was winding up, she and Jon had things to talk about, decisions to be made.

Their relationship was something special, she knew. Something real. And she knew Jon felt the same thing. He had mentioned the possibility of her working for the Omega Sector: Critical Response Division more than once.

It did sound as if she might be a better fit there. That her needs would be considered in a way they hadn't been at the Bureau office. And of course... Jon. She couldn't help smiling at the thought.

Another brave walker came toward her as she was about to make the turn off the beach for the road leading to the house. She smiled and waved when she realized it was handsome Dr. Trumpold from the hospital, the source of all Jon's jealously.

"Hi, Sherry," he said, smiling as he passed her.

Sherry was shocked he knew her name. Wait until she lorded this over Jon's head. She smiled at the thought.

But the truth was, no matter how handsome or successful Dr. Trumpold was, he still was no Jon Hatton.

She turned around for one last glance of the handsome doctor. He had stopped about fifty yards from her to look out at the sea. A gust of wind picked up and he slipped on the hood of the yellow sweatshirt he was wearing.

From this angle, the hood made Trumpold look like Fabio. As if he had long blond—

Sherry felt her stomach drop as a chill that had

nothing to do with the wind settled over her. She suddenly knew that whoever Jon had arrested today was the wrong guy.

Caroline hadn't seen blond hair in the quick glance she'd gotten of her attacker, although Sherry could very easily see why she would think so. What her friend had seen was the hood of a yellow sweatshirt pulled on the rapist's head.

Dr. Trumpold's head.

He turned and looked at Sherry, his smile eerily friendly.

Sherry dropped her shoes and ran toward her house, knowing he was following her.

Chapter Twenty-Five

It didn't take Jon and Brandon long in the interview room to figure out they had the wrong guy.

He was a punk, no doubt, with attitude to match his ridiculous hair. But someone with a high IQ, not to mention an understanding of how forensics worked so he didn't leave behind any DNA? Definitely not this guy.

And his hands certainly didn't match the profile. No swelling, no bruising, no marks whatsoever. Jon supposed that he could've used something else to inflict the extensive damage on Caroline, but she had mentioned his fist, so Jon didn't think so.

Jon wouldn't be surprised if this guy was guilty of a number of crimes, but he was not the monster who had committed the rapes.

They talked to him for a few more minutes, then left.

"Damn it." Jon considered attempting to put

a fist through the cement wall, but he knew the wall would win.

"There's no way that is the guy," Brandon agreed, his frustration clear. "They'll run DNA. I wouldn't be surprised if he's not responsible for some other crimes."

"I've got to talk to the captain, let him know. Based on my experience, that's not going to be pretty."

Brandon nodded. "Yeah, as hard as it is, we don't want people letting down their guard, thinking everything is safe if it's not."

Jon felt as if a hundred pounds had been placed on his shoulders. An arrest in this case, giving the people of Corpus Christi what they needed to feel safe, justice for Caroline and Jasmine and Tina and the other women... Jon had known he wanted to do that, but he'd had no idea how much he'd *needed* to.

Right now he needed to put his arms around Sherry. Just breathe her in.

He should be surprised by how much that need seemed to trump everything else but he wasn't. Although he would give anything to have it the other way around, at least arresting the wrong guy meant he had a few more days with her here. Days he'd be spending trying to convince her to move to Colorado Springs and take that job at Omega.

The captain could wait five minutes. Jon needed to see Sherry.

It didn't take long for him to find her note. He smiled. No, they wouldn't be celebrating tonight, but he still planned for there to be nakedness.

"What's that smile about?" Brandon asked.

"Nothing," Jon said. "Sherry. She went to see Caroline. Telling Zane and Caroline the news about this guy is going to be just as hard as telling Captain Harris."

"How about if I talk to the captain and you go tell them? Face-to-face might be better."

Jon agreed and tried calling Sherry on the way to the hospital, but it went to her voice mail. When he walked inside and found she wasn't with Zane and Caroline a little feeling of panic set in. He and Zane went out into the hallway to talk.

"I asked Sherry to go pick up some stuff for Caroline, to make her feel more comfortable," Zane said. "I gave her a key for the back door so she wouldn't disturb the crime scene in any way, although Forensics is done there."

"That's not what I'm worried about."

He tried Sherry's number again. Voice mail. He left a message this time.

"Hi, baby, it's me. It's very important that you call me the second you get this message, okay?"

"Jon, what's going on?"

"The suspect we have in custody is not the

right guy, Zane." Jon put his hand on the other man's shoulder. "I'm sorry. I was really hoping he was the one."

"You're sure?"

"Positive. I'm sorry," Jon repeated, knowing the words weren't enough.

Zane's curse was ugly. Jon couldn't agree more.

Jon's phone buzzed in his hand. Sherry. Relief coursed through him. "Hey, where are you?"

"Jon."

He could barely understand her over her labored breathing.

"He's right outside. I know he's going to kill me."

Jon was running down the hallway toward his car before she got to the second sentence.

SHERRY WASTED NO time running as fast as she could toward her house. If she was wrong and Dr. Trumpold wasn't the rapist, she would apologize profusely later.

But she knew she wasn't wrong. Too much of it made sense. He knew her, knew she was helping the police. And he was definitely smart enough to try to get away with it, as Jon and Brandon had profiled.

She had a good fifty-yard head start on him and knew that her survival depended on her reaching her house before he caught her. She yelled for help as she ran, but the wind drowned out her voice.

She thought of stopping at another house. Of pounding on a door for help. But if she chose a house where no one was home, that would be it for her—he'd be on her. She wouldn't have the chance to try a second house.

She had to make it to hers.

She could see her house now and dug her key chain out of her pocket as she ran, ignoring the pain of running on asphalt in bare feet. She turned sharply into her driveway, then up the three stairs of her small porch. She saw Dr. Trumpold out of the corner of her eye come sprinting into the driveway. She only had seconds.

She took a breath and focused on the keys. If she fumbled or dropped them now, he'd catch her. She sobbed in relief as the lock turned and she let herself in, slamming the door behind her and locking it. She heard Trumpold crash into it just a second later.

She knew she still wasn't safe. Too many windows...ways to get in.

She called Jon.

He answered after just one ring. "Hey, where are you?"

"Jon." She tried to get her breathing under control but couldn't. "He's right outside. I know he's going to kill me."

"Where are you, Sherry?"

"My house. He's here. I saw him on the beach. It's Dr. Trumpold. He's the rapist." She heard a loud thump against the door as Trumpold slammed himself against it. "He's breaking through the front door."

She heard Jon curse. "Sherry, get in your bedroom. Pull the dresser against the door. I'm on my way. Stay on the line with me."

The beating against the door stopped for a moment. "Sherry, I just want to talk. Explain why I did what I did. Open the door." Trumpold's voice sounded so reasonable from the outside.

"Sweetheart, get in your bedroom. Right now." Jon's voice on the phone drowned out the one outside the door.

Sherry did as Jon said. Immediately she could hear the pounding start on the door again.

"Okay, I'm in the bedroom. He says he just wants to talk."

Jon's bark of laughter held no humor whatsoever. "Fine. He can talk to you through the bedroom door. I'm ten minutes out."

They both knew Trumpold would be able to get into her bedroom before then.

Sherry rushed over to the dresser chest and pushed with all her might to move it in front of the door. At first it wouldn't budge, so she turned and put her back to it, pushing with her legs.

Instead of moving it fell over. But it still blocked the door and that was what counted.

"What happened? Are you okay?"

"Yes, I pushed the chest of drawers in front of the door."

"Good girl."

She couldn't hear Trumpold pounding on the outside door anymore. Was he already inside? Had he given up?

Her bedroom was almost unrecognizable to her, between the fallen dresser and her bed mattress completely missing. It looked as if it had been through a tornado.

"I don't know where he is," Sherry whispered to Jon. "It's quiet now. I'm scared."

"I know, baby. Stay focused. Look for things you can use as weapons if he gets in. Things you can throw. Hit him with. Candles, a lamp, hair spray to spray him in the eyes."

Sherry nodded and started gathering items. She was facing the door, waiting for Trumpold to start pounding.

And was totally unprepared for when the large window broke behind her and he came leaping through.

She was able to throw only one candle at him, which caught him on the shoulder before he was on her. Her cell phone fell to the floor and shattered into pieces.

"Everything law enforcement does tends to

be so predictable," Trumpold said, grabbing the lamp that she tried to swing at him and throwing it across the room. "For example, barricading a door. SWAT 101."

Had she really ever thought he was handsome? Now all she could see was a madman. "I thought you said you wanted to talk."

He shrugged. "I admit that wasn't the truth. I'm naughty." He laughed at his own joke. "It was worth a try, you know? You never know when someone is going to be stupid enough to just throw open the door."

He took a step closer to her and grabbed her by the hair, jerking her closer to him. "Like all those women. Especially your friend Caroline. How stupid was she?"

"She thought you were someone else," Sherry snarled, wincing as he pulled her hair again. She knew she had to keep him talking, but she also felt an ingrained need to defend her friend.

"Actually, I know that." Trumpold laughed again. "I overheard her talking on the phone to that cop love-me, love-me-not boyfriend of hers. 'Tomorrow. Three o'clock. Be there, Zane. You know you want to.'" He said it in a falsetto voice, mimicking Caroline.

He tugged on Sherry's hair again, bringing tears to her eyes. "The drama between those two. Seriously, it's like a soap opera. I waited to see if he would show up and he didn't."

He brought Sherry's face right up to his. "I did."

Sherry thought she might vomit.

"When I heard about the blond hair thing, I knew it was time to retire the yellow hoodie. Oops. That could've been a mess. But I'm so glad you were able to figure it out first."

Sherry knew he was going to kill her. There was no way he would let her live knowing what she knew. She began struggling in earnest.

He released her long enough to backhand her. She fell to the floor. He picked her up by the collar of her shirt.

"It's okay, because I realize now this whole punching with my fists thing is getting old. It hurts when you punch someone, you know? I've had to hide my hands for the past couple of days." He held them out where she could see his bruised and swollen knuckles. "Not an easy thing to do when you're a doctor."

He hit her again and Sherry spat blood, falling back to the floor.

"I've been bored with medicine for a while now, so leaving that behind and going to ground won't be a problem. I've been preparing for that contingency for months, in case law enforcement ever caught on to me. I'll pop back up somewhere else."

Sherry cringed away from him as he crouched to get close to her, straddling her hips. "You've shown me that it's infinitely more exciting to pursue and capture someone who *knows* me. Who *knows* what's going to happen. It means I have to kill them, but I think that's just the next step for me, don't you?"

Sherry just tried to control her terror to breathe enough air into her lungs and wait for a chance to get away.

He pulled out a wicked-looking, long-bladed knife and pointed it at the side of her neck. "Now, this is overkill, I know. It's, like, Crocodile Dundee big, right?" He chuckled again. "But I like it. It's kind of sexy. Knives are really a natural choice for me, since I've used scalpels for years at the hospital. I can kill quickly and painlessly or slowly and much less painlessly."

Sherry could feel the blade slide into her neck, the sharp sting. She stopped fighting. If she fought now he would just slice the blade across her throat.

"I'm sorry I don't have time to play with you longer." He kissed her cheek. "But I estimate the cavalry will arrive in about two minutes and I need to be gone before then."

Sherry felt the knife slice her deeper and tried to make one last desperate jerk away as Trumpold's body suddenly flew off hers.

Jon.

He had come in silently through the window and tackled Trumpold. Sherry brought her fingers up to her neck as she slid herself out of the way of where they were fighting. Her hand was soon soaked with her own blood.

That wasn't good.

Jon and the doctor were rolling on the floor. Jon had him in height, but Trumpold was strong and had the knife. Sherry winced as the Crocodile Dundee knife cut Jon in the biceps. Then she slumped against the dresser, feeling dizzy.

Jon got in a couple of good punches to Trumpold's face and Trumpold fell to the floor. Jon kicked away his knife and left him there on the floor, rushing to Sherry.

He pulled off his shirt.

"I don't think I can have sex right now," Sherry said. Her vision was getting a little fuzzy.

He pressed the shirt against her neck. He put his face right in front of hers. "Hey, you stay with me. I want a rain check on that offer, okay?"

Where he pressed against her neck hurt and she wanted to sleep but tried to stay awake.

She saw Trumpold get up behind Jon with that damn knife. She tried to form words but couldn't. She flung an arm out instead.

Jon turned and threw up his arm, stopping the knife from slicing into his back, although it cut deep into his arm. Trumpold raised the knife again. Jon shielded Sherry with his body, but she realized it was going to cost Jon his life. She weakly tried to push him out of the way as the knife sped toward his back again, but he wouldn't budge in his protection of her.

Then the doctor flew backward, away from them both, as a shot rang out from the window.

Sherry heard Zane's voice. "You're never going to hurt anyone again, you son of a bitch."

And everything fell to black.

Chapter Twenty-Six

Between the two of them they had eighty-six stitches.

Although Sherry's cut was deeper and she'd lost a lot more blood, Jon actually had the most stitches. But stitches wouldn't have helped either of them if Zane hadn't showed up when he had.

He'd followed Jon, with Caroline's prompting, and if he hadn't, both Jon and Sherry would be dead.

Jon had known he couldn't take the pressure off her neck wound without the danger of her bleeding to death, so stopping Trumpold's attack at his back would've been nearly impossible.

Zane's shot to Trumpold's chest hadn't killed him, unfortunately, but he'd be in prison for a long time. Sherry hoped that would give all the women he'd attacked a little peace. And she hoped Zane's role in stopping him would help the detective find some self-forgiveness, as well.

Sherry never planned to tell Zane what

Trumpold had said about Caroline's attack. Of how he'd waited for Zane to arrive and seized the opportunity to attack Caroline when Zane hadn't showed up.

Of course, she didn't have to tell Zane what Trumpold said. Zane had already been telling himself that since it happened.

Sherry's hospital room had been filled with Omega agents all day to the point where Dr. Rosemont finally had to kick them out. Brandon had been there, talking with her, asking questions, wanting to understand how Trumpold's brain worked. Liam had come back through town and crawled into her hospital bed with her, wrapping his arms around her as if they'd been lovers for years. Everyone else in the room had pretty much just rolled their eyes and ignored him.

Steve Drackett, director of the Omega Critical Response Division, had even made an appearance himself. He was checking on Jon, meeting with the mayor, but also wanted to make sure Sherry knew that she officially had a job waiting for her at Omega anytime she wanted to take it.

They were all gone now, but Jon hadn't left her the whole time. She'd woken in the hospital, fine once they'd been able stitch the wound and replace the blood she'd lost. He'd already gotten his own stitches by the time she was moved into a private room from the trauma unit. But she didn't need to stay. They were releasing her tonight.

Except she didn't really have anywhere to go. The beach house was a crime scene. Again.

"Are you about ready to go? Nurse Carreker said we're free whenever you're ready."

Most of the hospital was still reeling from the fact that Dr. Trumpold—a trusted doctor at their hospital—had been the rapist. Many of them had worked with the man every day for years.

"I don't really have anywhere to go. I guess I need to check into a hotel."

He put an arm around her as they walked down the hall toward the exit.

"That won't be necessary, if you don't mind staying with me for a few days."

"At the condo?"

"No, that was rented by Omega for work. I've gotten a different place."

He didn't offer any more information, so Sherry just walked with him as he led her to the car and then began to drive. It didn't take long to realize they were headed toward the beach.

"Is this okay?" he asked when he realized she understood where they were going. "I got a place. It's on the south end, not near your house or Caroline's. But I know you love the beach, and I wanted it to be a place that held good memories for you. For both of us."

Sherry nodded but didn't say anything. Honestly, she wasn't sure.

He drove in silence until they arrived at a tiny

little cottage just a couple of blocks from the waterfront. He put the car in Park and turned to her.

"You are owed two weeks of vacation, which starts now. The last week you worked for Omega, which they'll pay you for."

"But—"

"Director Drackett's orders, not mine. I had nothing to do with it."

Okay, she could handle that.

"I'm also taking two weeks of vacation and would like to spend it here with you, if you'll have me?"

She smiled at him and waggled her eyebrows. "Oh, I'll have you. Believe me, I'll have you."

"Good, because I had somebody go by and get your stuff from the house. It included that red bikini. I hope you will spend almost every hour of the next two weeks in that or less. Except for maybe your cowboy boots."

Sherry laughed and they opened the car doors. The sun was shining in grand Southern Texas fashion. She held her face up to it as she got out of the car. Jon came around to close the door behind her.

He backed her up against the car. "Just want to forewarn you, Ms. Mitchell, I also plan to spend the entire next two weeks convincing you to take that job at Omega. Because I don't think I can go back there without you."

Sherry wondered if she should tell him she already planned to take that job. Nah. It'd be more fun keeping him in suspense. "It sounds like you plan on handling me, Agent Hatton."

"Oh, very much so, Ms. Mitchell." He breathed soft kisses from her mouth along her jaw to her ear.

"I hope you'll do that correctly, Agent. Not overthink the situation too much."

"The only thing I'm in danger of overthinking is how to get you to fall in love with me like I am with you." He worked his lips back up to hers, then eased back so he could see the beautiful blue of her eyes.

She smiled. "No thinking necessary. Already falling."

She leaned in to his addictive warmth. She didn't think she'd ever feel too warm next to him. She loved the heat they generated.

And she knew. This house. This time. They were exactly what she needed.

He was exactly what she needed.

* * * * *

Look for more books in Janie Crouch's
OMEGA SECTOR: CRITICAL RESPONSE
*later this year. You'll find them wherever
Harlequin Intrigue books and ebooks are sold!*

LARGER-PRINT
BOOKS!

HARLEQUIN *Presents*®

**GET 2 FREE LARGER-PRINT
NOVELS PLUS 2 FREE GIFTS!**

PASSION
GUARANTEED
SEDUCTION

HPLP15

LARGER-PRINT BOOKS!

GET 2 FREE LARGER-PRINT NOVELS PLUS
2 FREE GIFTS!

HARLEQUIN®
Romance

From the Heart, For the Heart

YES! Please send me 2 FREE LARGER-PRINT Harlequin® Romance novels and my 2 FREE gifts (gifts are worth about $10). After receiving them, if I don't wish to receive any more books, I can return the shipping statement marked "cancel." If I don't cancel, I will receive 4 brand-new novels every month and be billed just $5.09 per book in the U.S. or $5.49 per book in Canada. That's a savings of at least 15% off the cover price! It's quite a bargain! Shipping and handling is just 50¢ per book in the U.S. and 75¢ per book in Canada.* I understand that accepting the 2 free books and gifts places me under no obligation to buy anything. I can always return a shipment and cancel at any time. Even if I never buy another book, the two free books and gifts are mine to keep forever.

119/319 HDN GHWC

Name	(PLEASE PRINT)	

Address		Apt. #

City	State/Prov.	Zip/Postal Code

Signature (if under 18, a parent or guardian must sign)

Mail to the **Reader Service:**
IN U.S.A.: P.O. Box 1867, Buffalo, NY 14240-1867
IN CANADA: P.O. Box 609, Fort Erie, Ontario L2A 5X3

Want to try two free books from another line?
Call 1-800-873-8635 or visit www.ReaderService.com.

* Terms and prices subject to change without notice. Prices do not include applicable taxes. Sales tax applicable in N.Y. Canadian residents will be charged applicable taxes. Offer not valid in Quebec. This offer is limited to one order per household. Not valid for current subscribers to Harlequin Romance Larger-Print books. All orders subject to credit approval. Credit or debit balances in a customer's account(s) may be offset by any other outstanding balance owed by or to the customer. Please allow 4 to 6 weeks for delivery. Offer available while quantities last.

Your Privacy—The Reader Service is committed to protecting your privacy. Our Privacy Policy is available online at www.ReaderService.com or upon request from the Reader Service.

We make a portion of our mailing list available to reputable third parties that offer products we believe may interest you. If you prefer that we not exchange your name with third parties, or if you wish to clarify or modify your communication preferences, please visit us at www.ReaderService.com/consumerschoice or write to us at Reader Service Preference Service, P.O. Box 9062, Buffalo, NY 14240-9062. Include your complete name and address.

LARGER-PRINT BOOKS!
GET 2 FREE LARGER-PRINT NOVELS PLUS
2 FREE GIFTS!

⟨H⟩HARLEQUIN®

super romance®

More Story...More Romance

YES! Please send me **The Montana Mavericks Collection** in Larger Print. This collection begins with 3 FREE books and 2 FREE gifts (gifts valued at approx. $20.00 retail) in the first shipment, along with the other first 4 books from the collection! If I do not cancel, I will receive 8 monthly shipments until I have the entire 51-book Montana Mavericks collection. I will receive 2 or 3 FREE books in each shipment and I will pay just $4.99 US/ $5.89 CDN for each of the other four books in each shipment, plus $2.99 for shipping and handling per shipment.*If I decide to keep the entire collection, I'll have paid for only 32 books, because 19 books are FREE! I understand that accepting the 3 free books and gifts places me under no obligation to buy anything. I can always return a shipment and cancel at any time. My free books and gifts are mine to keep no matter what I decide.

263 HCN 2404 463 HCN 2404

Name	(PLEASE PRINT)	
Address		Apt. #
City	State/Prov.	Zip/Postal Code

Signature (if under 18, a parent or guardian must sign)

Mail to the **Reader Service:**
IN U.S.A.: P.O. Box 1867, Buffalo, NY 14240-1867
IN CANADA: P.O. Box 609, Fort Erie, Ontario L2A 5X3